A
Penitent
Season

Ancilla L.

.....

Prologue

I have been following him around the house all evening. Each time he stands up, whether it is to fetch a glass of water from the kitchen or to go check on something, I go as well. I remain at a slight distance from him, I drag my feet because I am carrying the words I am unable to say with me. They're like load-bearing shackles attached to my ankles. He paces around the living room as he speaks into the phone and I vacillate in response to his path, consumed by this fugue state of need, like a zombie driven by a singular need. The last time I felt this way was the first time I felt this way, decades ago, before I understood why or how, I followed someone around the house, unaware as to why I wanted to beg them to beat me, but completely sure I had to ask because it was all that mattered in the world. I stop in my tracks as he disconnects the phone call and paces towards me.

"Why are you being my shadow?" He asks, gripping my chin in his hand.

"I need..." I start to say, and trail off because I have inadvertently uttered a complete sentence.

"I know what you need," he says, squeezing face inside his palm, "You will wait."

It is so hard to exist in this anticipatory state, like being the human embodiment of a raw nerve that is constantly exposed to the elements. Everything feels like it is directed at me — the wind like harpies come to carry me away, the nightfall as if it exists to foreshadow my tragedy and mine alone, the distant howling like a warning sign from a banshee of my own — I am so reactive to the entire world. It's the vulnerability, it will do something magical and horrible to the most sane individual. I offer so much of myself to him, I put no mechanisms of protection in place and even when I know for certain that all he will do is hurt me, it doesn't spur me to hide. I want him to be able to hurt me, I want it to be so easy for him, like biting a soft mint with your teeth. I want to be so known to him, he could shatter me in an instant. I want to pose no difficulty for him to defeat, I want to be the easiest victory of his life.

But he makes me wait.

I wait.

Hours later, as I kneel at his feet while he punches my arms and face, the waiting-period, formerly so capacious, seems to disappear into nothingness. As if I never experienced it at all. I sit quietly and still, I make myself small, as he flings his fists into my body without any concern as to my sentience. Sometimes it feels like he forgets there is a human being inside this flesh, I tell him that from time-to-time, most recently as he sewed me with a needle with the nonchalance of sewing cloth. I asked him if he realised that I could *feel* what he was doing to me, he told me not every realisation has to impact behaviour. But I misrepresent myself as well, at least to a certain extent, I am way less helpless than meets the eyes. This cruelty he afflicts upon me, it wasn't crafted by him alone. This state in which I sit before him, tremulous and terrorised, I begged for him to take me here. As I whimper and feel sorry for myself, in response to his blows, I know I would rather break than be excused. As I cry and snivel, I also lift my head right back up and place it exactly where he demands it be. I have to. I must. As he pulls his hands away from my body and rests them closer to his, I begin to panic.

"Please…" I whisper, the metallic taste in my mouth pouring over onto my lip.

"Please, what?" He asks, leaning so close to my face it feels like I could say my words directly into his mouth.

There is something I have been trying to say all evening. A sentiment with which I have chased him around our household, hoping he would recognise it without me having to succumb to the need to articulate it, but I know the moment has come. I cannot avoid the exposure of my truth anyway.

"Penance," I whisper.

This is the shameful, ugly truth of the suffering I want from him. Sometimes we do ourselves a favour and indulge in the explanation of a proximal cause.

Punish me because I forgot to stand up when you came into the room. Punish me because I broke a nail. Punish me because I came too close to pleasure. Punish me because I screamed when you demanded silence.

Some nights, though, the hifalutin constructs become impossible to keep up. The truth is some of us just need to be punished for who we are. There are no mistakes from which I need him to exonerate me, it is my original sin for which I must endlessly atone. I need to suffer because it is what I must believe I deserve. I will pretend to be sorry, so sorry, for every pedestrian lapse in meaningless adherence to arbitrary rules, but we know, we always know it isn't punishment I seek, I seek to repent. There is but one season our story, it is always Lent.

I am a sinner.

And he, my deliverer.

"Penance," he whispers back into my skin, I can sense his arousal, a thing so private, it feels like even I should not bear witness.

He leads me off the floor. In silence, he takes off all my clothes, this act should tell of lust but instead it feels like being prepared for slaughter. He lays me on the bed and prepares to assault my insides, it's where all the unbearable pain lives and it is the only pain I will always try to stop. I will cry and beg and apologise, but there are no lessons to learn here. This is not an apologue. This is not catharsis. It isn't punishment.

Yet I make amends.

"I'm sorry," I tell him as his fingers prepare to penetrate me in the most gruesome act of violation I can imagine.

"I'm not here to forgive you, I'm here to make an example of you," he says and he tightens the noose inside me, "I'm not your priest, my love, I'm your executioner."

He is.

I would fight for justice if this wasn't exactly what I deserve. His fingers reach inside me and I cry out as my legs reflexively snap together. He pries them open and assaults me harder. Faster. Until I feel my insides relent and accept my fate.

"Penance can hardly be accomplished in one night, you know," he says, "Maybe you need a season of repentance."

He wants me to have a Lent. He wants to turn a fortnight of being around and off work into a penitent season for me. It makes sense.

Let it be Lent, then.

Please.

Day 1

I stayed awake a great deal of the night. He fell asleep moments after we got in bed. I could still feel him dripping out of my cunt when he started to snore. My jaw was still throbbing, my arms still so incredibly sore from the punching and my insides still raw from the assault of his fingers and his cock. When he got in bed beside me, I was still cowering, hiding my body inside the curvature of my shoulders to thwart any more attacks; when he reached over to move my hair aside and kiss me, I flinched and squealed. Sometimes, I am unsure as to how to explain to people that trauma responses are the most romantic thing your partner can give to you, they reach deeper than other responses. They reside in the same realm as evolutionary fears and heart-rates that elevate in response to adrenaline, responses like that are meant to obey humanity, but instead, they obey him. When he gives me trauma, he brands my psyche. It's like a tattoo on my soul, an emotional memory so strong and significant I couldn't forget it if I tried.

"You poor girl," he told me before he turned around to sleep, "This fortnight is going to be so difficult for you."

I spent most of the night wondering if I was comforted by that declaration or confronted by it. Every couple of hours, I'd wish I could wake him up and offer more of my body up for hurt, then I'd shudder at my need and try to force myself back to sleep. When I woke up I hadn't been asleep for very long, I shook out of somnolence because he was stroking the hair off my face and just as he leaned in to tuck it behind my ear, I began to cry.

"I'm sorry, please," I muttered even before my eyes were completely open.

It took a few minutes for me to realise that dawn had just broken, he hadn't just been beating me, he wasn't about to hit me again, we had just woken up to a new day. He kissed me on my forehead and I placed my palm against his chest.

"I love you," he whispered into my head, stroking my hair and holding me against his chest.

"I love you as well," I sobbed into his fuzzy skin that tickles my nose as much as it provides the comfort of a terrible, ratty blanket of my youth.

"It's going to be okay," he said, as I pulled away and prepared to get out of bed.

"Is it, really?" I asked, grazing my jaw with the tips of his fingers.

"Well, for me, it will be okay for me," he said, shaking his fingers from the grips of mine and squeezing my face.

"And for me?" I asked, looking down at the sheets, unable to bear his gaze.

"A penitent season, my love," he said with the finality of a guillotine, "It's what you deserve."

...

There was a terrible poster on the mirror in my grandmother's dressing room. It was yellow and in a garish font it read: *Marriage is not a word, it is a sentence.*

They meant it to be funny in the way that that generation thinks it's funny to spend your life with someone you hate and casually reference that fact constantly. For the longest time, I didn't understand the poster and when I did, it made me angry. Then I fell in love and it took on a whole new meaning.

His love is a sentence.

And my imprisonment is my homecoming.

I think about that poster a lot.

...

He came to me an hour before lunch and dragged me from my desk to the edge of the bed. Normally, he wouldn't interrupt my work and as a matter of habit I would never be so accessible while I am working that I can be reached. There are aspects about my life about which I am completely private and that exclusion includes the people closest to me. All of my work requires exposure of some kind, It's vital I be able to enforce some kind of insulation. I find it comforting to love a person who doesn't feel entitled to the entirety of me but especially to love a person who understands that the things I keep to myself aren't something I am doing to him. I find it liberating to love a man to whom I can declare that I am doing something about which I can tell him nothing, even if I leave town for several days to pursue it, and have him accept that answer as adequate information that requires no further explanation. I would do the same for him, in some ways, there are parts of him he doesn't want to experience in my presence. I relish this lack of pretence. We believe separateness to be a necessarily bad thing but it isn't, this lack of expectations around how a relationship should look is why my marriage isn't a sentence, it's a constant delight.

However, for a short period, I've given myself permission to be distracted, to prioritise pleasure and relaxation over goals, schedules and routine. It's a celebration. I realise I have a problem and it has been more and more clear to me over the past year, I put off celebrating and push the goal each time I achieve one, it has led me to being terribly cruel to myself in terms of how much joy I am allowed to experience. It's about the award. I won one and I feel horrible about having won it. For months I couldn't tell anyone I was even nominated, I only told my husband I was on the shortlist a week after they told me and I cried from shame when I did win. For days I have been avoiding taking people's calls because I know why they are calling and I feel sick to my stomach. I couldn't even tell my stepson because I knew he would want to buy me a present or throw a party but I know something no one else knows, I know in my bones that I do not deserve this. I haven't done enough, I haven't worked hard enough, I haven't suffered enough. Life has been too easy for me, I shouldn't be rewarded.

I have a problem.

So, I have decided to address it by teaching myself to relax and to celebrate an achievement even if it feels fraudulent and makes me uncomfortable. In the interest of celebration, I have allowed myself to be swayed by my husband's vacation insofar as I will prioritise enjoyment over responsibility, goals and duty for two weeks. I will succumb to romance and whimsy. My mother said to me recently that she felt like she had made a mistake by raising me to be so career-focused because if she hadn't, at least I would have learnt to have fun and relax, and not have grey hair at 31. It is mostly the grey hair that bothers her, I think. She is worried I will look older than my husband who is a decade older than I am, in fact, she believes I already do, and if I don't immediately put a lot of aloe vera on my face and take more vacations, all hell shall break loose because some people may think that I look old. God, I love that insane, strange woman, and she is right that her upbringing is part of why I cannot relax.

And so I have resolved to do it.

It makes sense to me that I want to indulge not in travel or sloth in pursuit of relaxation, but in lust. We should be allowed vacations of lust. It is easier than anything else for me to allow myself indulgence into this state where my sexuality gets to be primary, and in this state, when he pulls me from my desk, I am able to follow. I was able to forget what I was doing, drop it without notice and worry that I would forget to take care of it when I went back to it, and follow him even though night hadn't fallen, I wasn't allowed yet by my own constraints of how life should function to be free, distracted by pleasure or allowed to shirk responsibility. It has to be a vacation of penance for me to take one, I suppose.

He sat me down on the edge of the bed and squeezed the swollen bits of both my arms. The skin was still warm from the previous night, the bruises hadn't even risen to the surface. He brought a spry little cane from the closet and began to run it over the swollen bits of my biceps.

"I'm sorry," I said as I felt him take aim on my left arm, "I deserve to be punished."

I don't. Maybe I do. Maybe there is no such thing. I don't know anymore. I just wanted to declare my state of repentance, I just wanted to reinforce this state of being a sorry creature who knows no pleasure but to suffer. It knows no ballads of lust but amends whispered shamefully into the silence. It knows nothing of what it ought to feel only that it feels sorry and it must. If I insist on finding meaning only in suffering, the least I can do is commit to a discipline of suffering.

"Good," he said, approvingly, "Hope is a fool's crutch, you are not a fool, are you?"

I am.

By every definition of the word including the one about which you must write essays as a student of literature, I am a fool, but I am not deluded. Hope is for other people, hope is not for me. I don't think of my world, nor my future, in terms of better or worse, I have no need for hope. I wouldn't know what to hope for. I'd like to believe that. He struck my arm with ferocity that may not have felt so harsh if I hadn't already been hurting, but I suppose I should get used to that. If you're going to go to the penitentiary of pain for fourteen days, you are going to run out of healed, unblemished flesh to assault. All these beatings and terrible things I assume will follow will have to be layered over the beatings and terrible things of yesterdays. Does it sound like I lament? It's a misdirect, I moan in lament.

The beating was short and harsh. I went back to my desk with a twitch in my left arm. It passed after a few minutes and a glass of water. He stared at me from across the room as I typed into my keyboard, I pretended I didn't know he was watching me, but I could feel his gaze touching me. Wrapping its tentacles around my throat to choke out the tears building inside my chest.

I pretended he couldn't see me.

...

He fucked me with the glass dildo in that strange hour of the early evening after I finish my work and before the kid comes back from school. This act he performs, it is so specific in its purpose and compulsive in its execution, that it always feels dirtier than it should. In the grand scheme of things fucking my cunt with an object that actually belongs in there is so tame, but it is the worst. No one knows, or maybe I just feel no one understands, exactly how terrible it is. He doesn't fuck me with things to turn me on, he does it to keep me in a state of soreness and pain. He fucks me with his fingers like an assault and before it heals he fucks me with something else so that by the time he tells me to bend over so he can fuck me with his cock, I am already so used-up and afraid, it takes merely the gentle threat of a thrust to render me incoherent. The way he fucks me is how he, over the years, broke me down to his specific set of sexual functions for me.

It's appalling.

I cannot live without it.

...

He wouldn't move the hair off my face. It tickled my nose and he could see me trying to use my shoulder to move it off my face but he wouldn't help me. I find that is more cruel than the beating he was delivering to my breasts at the time, it was the breakdown of the social contract of sadomasochism, he is supposed to move the hair off my face when my hands are too tied up to do it myself. I did not complain, though. Mostly because I think there was marginal kindness in the way he tied my hands to the pull-up bar in the doorway. He cuffed them together but to secure them to the bar he used a somewhat elastic section of chord, it allowed me to relax my shoulders from time-to-time. It made me less afraid of losing my footing and later, when my feet started to go numb from standing there for so long, it allowed me to stoop lower without hurting myself.

But that was the extent of the kindness.

He beat my breasts with a shoe-horn and I wailed out loud twice during the hour. Both times he hit me harder and chided me for misbehaving. Both times I resolved not to do it again and soon enough, I wasn't really able to do it again. I was so exhausted, my head started to stoop and rest on my shoulder. My eyes started to close and the atmosphere got so languorous, I worried I would doze off between blows and be woken up with the most jarring cracking sound against my skin. I would have begged for mercy, not that it's a guarantee of getting it, but begging usually gets me to mercy faster, but I am fairly certain I am not allowed to beg for mercy. You cannot be repentant and still beg for mercy, right? It did end eventually, he untied my arms and pointed me to the bed.

"On your back," he said to me, "Spread your legs."

I am scared that he is going to put his fingers inside me every single night. I could still feel their impact from the previous night, still lingering inside me. I fear nothing like I fear his fingers inside me. As he moved between my legs, he stroked the inside of my thigh and perhaps as an unfortunate force of habit I tightened the muscles in my hips to keep my legs from opening up further, he pushed against the tension in my hip and maybe, just maybe, I pushed back. I felt like I hadn't moved at all.

"Are you resisting me?" He asked, leaping towards my face and squishing it inside his palm.

I panicked. I apologised in a panic. I wasn't, I really wasn't resisting him but I know not to explain myself, he doesn't care for explanation, even if I have the best one, it will only get me beaten harder so I just apologised and spread my legs. He pushed his fingers inside me, their insidious path lead to the same places as always, but I never get used to it. I will never get used to it. I am a stupid, useless girl. As he fucked me with his fingers, I got to the place where all of it started to make sense again, as the senseless suffering of my insides took over everything, I found the desire to remain there.

"Thank you for punishing me," I said to him.

I always know that's what he wants to hear, but I can never say it until it wants to be said.

...

He held me close and kissed me a lot before we went to bed. He touched my body, perhaps even as an act of desire and not in a manner so punitive as the rest of the day, but I could not adjust to the comfort of his kindness. It felt like a threat. A lie. A shelter erected only to lure weary travelers and rob them. He assured me he would only hurt me again the next day, that I didn't have to worry about the intervening night, I could bury myself in his warmth.

"Am I a bad slave?" I asked him, I never ask such questions, they mean nothing to me, but vulnerability and exhaustion will turn you into a different person, one that seeks comforts it didn't even know it wanted.

"Yes, you are," he said, not even appearing to think about it.

I would bury myself in his warmth, but I suspect it's a grave.

...

Day 2

I overslept this morning. I have no idea how it happened. I woke up at four-thirty and I stayed awake for almost an hour, writing and watching him sleep, then I dozed off with my phone in my hand. Either my alarm didn't go off or I didn't hear it, but either way, this is insanity to me. This is only the second time in my life that I can recall oversleeping. I woke up and ran out of bed. The kid was alarmed that I had managed to get off schedule and I am a little afraid now that relaxation will make me unproductive, unreliable and stupid. I know that is the wrong approach but honestly, I think people who have the same personality as me will understand how difficult it is to believe that things will work out without your active, back-breaking effort. Everybody loves to poke fun at us and maybe even feel sorry for us because we appear to be incapable of enjoying life (which is not true, some us do genuinely find our pleasure in the study of verbs and the solutions of crossword puzzles), but when the building is on fire they all come looking for us. Why do you think we can help when the building is on fire? It's because we've been driven, anal and prepared on a daily basis. It's a big deal to us when we oversleep. We cannot be sanguine in this place. If it seems anodyne, that is only to you.

...

He fucked me. It was unpleasant. However, that is not as relevant as the fact that the energy seems different between us. It is not quite like living with a parent nor really even living with your master, it's like living with your executioner. Your jailer. Your warden. Your less-than-benevolent priest. I feel emboldened to prostrate my penance before him. I want to crawl on the floor until my knees bleed so he can see that I know what I deserve. I want to latibulate, every single time he finishes up with me, I want to beg him to force me into the corner and leave me there to think about how terrible one would have to be to deserve this treatment. This feeling of deserving, it circumvents dread in a way. When he hurts me, I often get to the place of fear eventually, but there is a difference in the flavour of this torture. I feel less afraid, more unfortunate. Less fearful, more wretched. Even though he doesn't always stop, I always beg him to stop freely if that is what I want, but now I feel disallowed from feeling like I have that right. It feels like I cannot even ask.

I have been thinking about why I wouldn't beg for mercy last night. When a sinner brings herself for absolution, she may beg for mercy, because the forgiveness of God seems to come from a place of mercy. There seems to be this idea that you can *almost* earn it, but the final measure of forgiveness is a result of the grace of God. Their mercy. More than you deserve. I haven't brought myself for absolution though. This is not that part of the story yet. I don't think that part of the story exists in my version of the tale. I have brought myself for atonement and in atonement there seems to be no room for mercy, it seems not just distasteful to ask but defeating of the purpose.

I cannot ask for mercy.

I spent the morning working and when I came back into the bedroom, he was sitting upright against the headboard and reading.

"What are you reading?" I asked him.

"You," he said.

It is always thrilling to hear anyone say that.

"Do you like it?" I asked.

He pushed the quilt off his legs and brandished the erection in his shorts. It was less thrilling to see that, but only because it reminds me that my words are worthwhile for his pleasure, I don't think I need to be reminded of that. I want to strangle my ego and all pride until they are blue in the face, I want to feel the life slip out of those facets of me. He snapped his fingers and pointed at his cock, I crawled onto the bed and reached inside his clothes to put him in my mouth. I feel ashamed when he needs me for things, I wish I could give him a mouth more worthy. I feel like I shouldn't be allowed to see him in states of arousal or need, they feel so private and my presence in them feels so underserved, but I do love sucking his cock. It's the scent that intoxicates me, the first time I ever put my face into his crotch, I was hooked on it like a drug. I sniff and yearn like a rabid animal.

I sucked his cock while he read, it was so different from when I sucked his cock the day before, he was trying to bore a hole in my head that day, but today, he was happy to lay back, while I savoured every inch of his cock. I let myself get lost in it, the skin so soft against my lips yet so taut and firm. There is a tactile pleasure to feeling it inside your mouth.

"Take your clothes off," he said, kicking my face to move me aside.

Until then I had forgotten that I was preparing the weapon of my own destruction, perhaps allowing myself to believe that I could drink him down my throat and escape the penetration into my cunt. The reminder was like being doused in a batch of noisome water, the kind that remains in vases when flowers die. I began to undress, slower than I should have, but quick enough that he wasn't perturbed.

"Just lose the pants, actually," he said, standing against the bed and waiting, "What do I need with your body, it's not like I'm about to derive any pleasure from seeing it."

I pulled my pants to the floor and tried to avoid thinking about those words. This pithy, unnecessary commentary isn't for the moment, he leaves it in my brain to fester, it will have its moment of relevance, probably when I feel most safe from it. He fucked me hard and quick, holding my wrists behind my back while I sobbed into the bed. What a thing it is, to fear being fucked by the person you love most, I wouldn't change it for the world.

After he finished, I stayed there for a while.

And when I stood up, I fell.

...

He called me disappointing after he beat my back with his belt. I stood up from my desk and went to the bathroom, and when I came back he was standing beside the bed with his belt folded up in his hand.

"It's that time of the day," he said to me, gesturing to the expanse of sheets in front of him, "Take off your shirt."

That time of day. This man is so pedantic that in one day he has created an altered routine of pleasure and in it, at 1300 hours, he must beat me. I think I can predict the routine with some accuracy already: sexual torment in the morning, beat me in the afternoon, threatening and foreshadowing elements of torture in the evening in the evening then beat me more elaborately again at night and conduct some psychological warfare right before I fall asleep. I could be wrong, he will probably alter the routine at some point. I wonder if this is too much torture for one person to endure every day, I suppose I shall find out.

I am surprised by how hard he whipped my back with his belt. Usually, he will beat me for a couple of hours with an implement like that, but in forty minutes this afternoon he reduced me to a complete mess. I think I take for granted the comfort of being walked into the pain gently. When he started, he was already at a hundred, that's how he has been since yesterday. He won't give me a little time to warm up, he won't give me a moment to adjust, I didn't realise how much that really helps now that he won't do it anymore. It was just forty minutes, 2400 seconds, yet it was the worst beating I have ever gotten from that belt. I was crying. For the most part, when I am being hurt, I think about how much more of it I want, but all I could think about this afternoon was how much I wanted him to stop. There was a moment, a moment I suppressed under a silent scream directed into the memory foam, when I was indignant, I almost expressed some annoyance and anger out loud. As if I had room to take issue with beating a person this way, but as soon as that moment passed, I felt worse than before. That sentiment still feels like a single hair stuck to my skin in front of my eye, I keep trying to push it aside, and failing that, I keep trying to explain to myself that a single strand couldn't possibly cause me this much distress, but it does. It's debilitating to my calm.

I know what I have done. If I had expressed my indignation out loud, I wouldn't be writing right now, I would still be bent over that bed having the life beaten out of me, and I understand the temptation to say that I don't need to be checked for something I didn't do, but I know him too. I know he would feel the same way as I do. It's because when he punishes me for behaving in ways that resemble human, it's not just for manifesting those reactions, he is doing it for even thinking about them. He would punish me as hard for thinking of screaming or wanting to do it, as he would for actually doing it. I know that if I tell him of my mental repose from exemplary behaviour, he would be immediately displeased and now it feels like something I am keeping.

I noticed I process and manifest a lot of my pain through my hands. There had to be something. It has to go somewhere and since he has criminalized screams, condemned audible whimpers, stigmatised moving, restricted crying and is actively looking down upon breathing too hard, my hands are all that remain. I grip, squeeze, scratch, hold and rub things a lot when he beats me. I was holding onto a pillow this afternoon and I wondered what I would do if he forced me to keep my hands perfectly still and outstretched while he hurt me. Even the thought was mortifying, but only because it carries such inevitability. My favourite thing about him, about us, is that the source of ideas is a nebulous mire, I can never tell if I am responsible for something he is doing to me, or he is. Am I responsible for the pain that will befall me when I tell him I had *thoughts* of revolt or is he? Whose decision will that punitive act have been? I cannot figure it out.

I will tell him, though. I know that. I will put it on the list. The list was my idea, all lists are always my idea. Essentially if it's an idea that involves writing something, it's my idea. I proposed I make a list every day of things for which I think I should be punished. It's a psychological experiment. I want to find my guilt. Not things he would want to punish me for, not things based on arbitrary rules that are applicable in power exchange relationships, but things that drive the sense of guilt that led me to this place where I am so sorry that I had to express it by turning my suffering into penance, into a season, an art project and all of my sex life. It's a bit extreme even for sex-and-kink positive mindsets. I figured by associating the telling markers of arousal to a specific feature of guilt-diagnosis, I will be able to identify the repository of my guilt. The guilt I feel about experiencing an emotion akin to anger, it is not a construct borne from my arousal, the narrative around it, that's all colour and masturbatory fodder, but the source of the guilt is what I want to find. I am uncomfortable with feeling angry, it feels like a sickness in my body and even short bouts of completely non-destructive anger that I don't even express and reason through instead makes me feel like I should have a pill and a cleanse to rid myself of that feeling. Punishment is cleansing. Or at least, I have convinced myself of that, and I'm keeping that belief because if you had as much fun as I do getting my ass beat and my soul crushed, you would keep it too.

I screamed once at the end of his beating. He hit me so hard I lost my footing even though I was bent over with my feet firmly on the floor. My guilt about that is not as potent or diagnostic, I still want to be punished for it, and he did, but it won't make the list.

He called me disappointing because I screamed once and told me he hoped I wouldn't be as disappointing later at night. I think his blade is too trenchant for its own good, or mine. It's too trenchant for my good.

...

When we were putting lunch together in the kitchen, I was so overwhelmed by an emotion so granular, I don't think they've made a term for it yet.

"I feel like I cannot stand on my feet around you," I told him as he brought cutlery from the other end of the kitchen.

"Crawl, then," he said.

It was all the permission I needed to drop to the floor. It has never felt so much like home before, the sheer act of being on my hands and knees felt like being touched by a lover in places only they can find on your body. Places that disappear when lovers who discovered them are gone. He walked over to where I was, beside the counter with the plates and he kicked me out of the way.

"If you're going to crawl, do not get in my way," he said, so unimpressed with my gestures of subservience, they feel completely selfish.

I crawled behind him to the table. I was hurt when he asked me to sit on the chair and eat.

...

I asked him not to touch my cunt with his fingers except to hurt it on the insides. He was fucking me with a dildo and he stopped for a second to graze my skin and my clitoris. It felt so wrong. It's not that I don't like it when he touches me like that, it's quite the contrary, it's the only sexual thing he does to my body that makes me feel like he sees me as a human being, a lover even, not just his slave.

But I feel like I should have to give up my pleasures.

I commit a little too well to constructs, I'm afraid. I cannot engage in a minor dalliance, it has to be a complete affair that leaves my world annihilated. That's why I do any of it. It would be counter-productive to choose not to commit. It seems like Lent requires a sacrifice of my pleasures and his fingers are one of the most potent sources of my pleasure. I could give up orgasms but for me that is like a teetotaler giving up alcohol. It's not something I do often and when I do there is almost nothing for me there. His fingers though, when they touch me and tease me, allowing me to actively swim in the vast expanses of arousal in all of its shades, that's where I derive all of my direct, sexual pleasure. I should have to give that up.

So, I asked.

He agreed immediately. Usually, he may have chided me for chiming in with my own idea at that moment and in contradiction to what he was doing but I think he sees something I see as well. Penance is internally driven. It's not about what he thinks I deserve, it's also about what I think I deserve.

This is what I deserve.

...

I pulled my own hair. I hadn't done that in a very long time. I was lying on the floor, on my back, and he was kicking me with his boots. He walked around me in circles, stepping on my hands, grinding into my toes, kicking my arms, sides, thighs and shoulders, stepping on my breasts and my cunt. I screamed at the second kick, it was not possible for me not to do it. He has kicked me many times before, in the same boots too, but never so hard. There wasn't even an intervening period where I could pretend to enjoy it. He has stepped on my hands and feet before but never with all of his weight. It felt like he was crushing them. *Did you even know hands could bruise?*

It was still unacceptable to him that I screamed. He kicked me four times in response to my scream, each time on my left thigh and I thought for sure that I would die. I made it to the third kick in relative silence but at the fourth one I screamed so loudly the dog came over to our bedroom and started scratching at the door. He laughed at me and told me that no one was coming for me before reassuring the dog through the door. He leaned down over me and slapped me. Twice on each side and once in the mouth with the back of his hand, the way his knuckle hit my lip caused it to swell up instantly. *Did you even know lips could bruise?*

I started crying in the first five minutes of his violent assault. *Five minutes.* It started right after he hit me in the face, I had taken for granted that he wouldn't do that for a few days because my face still hasn't healed from Sunday. The thing about being slapped and hit in the face a lot is that it's not the potential bruises nor the swelling that is the real long-term problem, it's that each intense facial-beating fucks your skin up for at least five days and the pain of a bruise has nothing on the pain that lasts, the kind that's bone-deep, and it takes time to heal from both of those things. The moment I realised he wouldn't give me the simplest of comforts, cut me the most humane of corners, I really couldn't keep it in anymore. One slap in the jaw and I could feel it all the way inside my mandible. *Did you even know bones could bruise?*

I didn't scream after that. Well, I didn't scream out loud but I screamed in whispers. It's the most pathetic sound, it's a whisper but it's coming from harrowing depths of disbelief and terror. I suppose I should be grateful that he allowed me to scream in whispers. Sometimes it is hard to believe that he will keep going even though it is so, so clearly visible that I cannot take it. It breaks my heart a little every single time I realise exactly how cruel and cold he can be. Despite the fact that I cried so many tears, I got the floor wet, he didn't stop for one sympathetic moment. Despite the fact that I went hoarse from silent screaming, he didn't reduce the intensity of the pain he was causing me. *Did you even know a heart could bruise?*

I do.

I know exactly what it looks like when it does. He hit me so hard in my shoulder, I put my hands together in prayer to beg, he decided it was unacceptable that I aspire to mercy so he hit me again, in the same spot, again and again, until the only course of action that remained to me was to pull my own hair. I pulled so hard, I plucked them out of the roots.

For one fleeting moment, I wished I had the will to run away and lock myself in the bathroom, but I didn't, so I pulled my hair to distract from his pain.

"Let me do that for you," he said, displeased with the distraction I had found.

He pulled my hair.

Did you even know the scalp could bruise?

...

Day 3

I am not sure if he woke me up in the middle of the night, if I woke him up in the middle of the night or if it happened before we went to bed. My issue is about semantics, really, I don't know if this should have been the ending of my last chapter or it's okay for it to be the beginning of this one. The intervening night is hard to classify. When we went to bed he was very, very kind to me. I know why. It's because I went quiet after the beating on the floor, I don't think anyone in my life knows how to handle that silence from me. It never happens either. I can be quiet for the hours that I am being fucked, tortured or beaten, I can be quiet when I am writing, but immediately after, I will start talking again.

I couldn't talk last night.

He asked me afterwards if there was something I wanted to say about what had happened and I told him that I had a lot to say, but that's all I said for the next few hours. I was in shock. The panic I experienced when he was kicking me and crushing my fingers, toes and face last night, reminded me of the panic of a different period of my life. I actually felt the desire to get up and run. I haven't experienced the reflex to flee in a long time. I am not sure how I feel about that. I have also not experienced this level of intensity in a while. I do not mean I have not been experiencing intensity, honestly, intensity is a habit that is entrenched bone-deep and evenly across every aspect of oneself. It's like my friend Bel. She had a meal once after smoking her first joint ever, then she started smoking joints before every meal to enhance the experience and soon enough Bel couldn't eat if she hadn't had a joint first because food just didn't feel like enough of an experience without it. Intensity is placebo for would-be junkies.

But last night was an intensity that scratched a realm of fear I had forgotten. A panic to get him to stop because I sensed a mortal fear and the constant reinforcement of the knowledge that I couldn't get him to stop. I kept wishing with every single blow that it would be the last, I cried so much, but he just wouldn't stop. I don't remember when he did, or why, but I was so grateful I leapt at his feet to thank him for it. The rest of the evening passed in my silence and his attempts to ensure that I was okay, I was okay, I think. I was just quiet. Then at some point in the night, I found myself tossing and turning. Yearning to be touched like a person. The humming in my cunt was fatidic, like it foretold a chronicle I had already written.

"I wish you could touch me," I found myself saying at some point.

He put his hands across my abdomen and stroked my skin. I moaned even though there was no pleasure to be found in that part of my body. I wanted his fingers on my cunt so badly, in only two days I found myself in a place where the thing I had given up was so difficult to resist. How weak and pathetic.

"Not for another twelve days," he told me, "You won't feel my fingers to do anything but hurt your cunt, for twelve more days."

Someone has to be strong for the sake of the construct. Surely, that's insanity. For two people to be denied at the same time, one to be denied the pleasure they seek and for the other to be denied the fulfillment of the urge to placate and pacify their partner in a state of hurt, who does that serve exactly? I don't know, yet I am glad he wouldn't touch me.

"If you can't touch my cunt to pleasure me, hurt it please," I begged, "I'll take the harshness of your fingers inside me just to feel them."

I didn't know I meant it, but I meant it.

"I feel so sorry for you," he said, pulling the covers off me and repositioning himself to be able to stab me with the flesh-toned knives attached to his hands.

"May I get on my stomach please?" I asked.

I don't know why it had to be that way but it did. I turned over to my stomach and lifted my hips upwards so he could access my hole with ease. He put his fingers inside me and waded around a little bit. I don't know what it is about being penetrated in that position, it makes everything hurt more. I have forgotten what it's like to be fucked on my back or why anyone would do it, but usually, when he puts his fingers or a dildo in me, I literally cannot stand it when I am on my stomach. It's a physical pain so extreme, I start to shake in anticipation. Still, I seem unable to accept there will ever be enough suffering for me.

"Please," I beg him as he fucks me with his fingers, slower than the last time he did it.

"Please what?" He asks.

"Please master," I muster from the depths of my shame, "Please punish."

And then he did.

Who did that serve?

...

I think doing edibles changed my personality. Look, I know how that sounds but hear me out. I've been struggling for a while with the right to recreation and enjoyment. I believe I do not deserve it. I believe that if I am not completely functional and productive at all times, I do not have the right to exist. You know that hour between the gym and having dinner? You could sit around in your house and just talk to people. Or the concept of hobbies? Like painting a picture but not because you want to turn that into a business? I don't get that. You could be shelling peas or responding to some e-mails in that time. I'll smoke a joint, right? But all I do when high is work or write. Relaxation is okay until it is still productive but doing edibles quietened the part of my brain that is hard-wired to constantly seek tasks and wrest responsibility for myself from the entire world. It was amazing and it had a lasting impact. It's been ten days or more, but I still feel a level of calm, maybe it's because I didn't actually believe prior to this experience that being relaxed was real. I really just thought everyone was saying it but not really feeling it. Felt like a scam, truly. Then I actually experienced it and now I think everyone wasn't lying and I am a real moron.

This state of calm, though, it has enabled me to think about and confront issues I had previously deemed unproductive. I classify my emotions in this way as well. I refuse to wallow in them. Either there exists in a situation an action you can take that presents a solution or there is nothing to be done so you just have to live with it, but there seem to be other options if you think of yourself as a person entitled to a little care and consideration for your pain. Even unproductive emotions can leave an impact on you.

Who knew.

...

Droplets of blood from my back splashed onto my arms as he flogged me. I was unperturbed when I saw the flogger because, come on, it's a flogger, what is the worst thing you can do with a flogger? They're like masochist massages. Your shoulders will always be more sore than my back if you flog me. Except he brought a scalpel and cut the word "repent" into my back before he beat me. Way to bring a knife to a gunfight. I respect his commitment to weakening the opponent before stepping into the arena. Not that I think of myself as his opponent.

This is his style is what I mean. When we first got together and the "play" was a lot more physical than it was contextual and emotional, he would run a sharp wire-brush over my skin before he cut it with a blade because that made it worse, or he'd carve me with a dull knife before he took a belt to me. It is the same thing as what he does to my cunt for days before he fucks it. He changes the conditions of the terrain so that a little bit of strife feels like a lot. A five-kilometer walk is not that bad, but if you have to do it through snow, it could be a real ordeal. A flogger is nothing, but it can be terrible if you're cut and bleeding.

The blood splashed all over me as he beat me. It was beautiful and it was the kind of pain to which my reflexes are already eroded so I was able to be quiet and poised the way he likes me to be. I've used the word eroded twice today. I said it to him a couple of hours ago because I was sitting at the dining table and complaining about being hungry, willing the stove to cook the food faster, and he suggested he distract me by hurting me. I stood up instantly and walked to the room. He said he was surprised I didn't bat for food, or momentary respite, that I didn't even give him a look or take a beat before I walked towards the bedroom. I don't think it's surprising at all. My defenses are eroded. They were on the way to erosion but last night hastened the process and as he beat me on my bloody back this afternoon I realised exactly what is different about him within this construct. I am testing the limits of my guilt and he is testing his extremes.

Each beating is the worst possible rendition of itself because my commitment to penance means that he doesn't have to cater to the caveats of my masochism which in varying degrees of play depend on what is happening between us. My misery is contingent upon his extremes and so he isn't doing the things he usually does to make my pain last longer, he doesn't have to start gently and escalate, he doesn't have to be mindful of my emotional state or well-being to the goal of stability (which is entirely by design and not at all by lack of consideration), he doesn't have to use only the tools I really like, he doesn't have to go slowly, he doesn't have to spread the pain out. In fact, the opposite of all of those is the fastest path to suffering, not pleasurable suffering of the style of "*I own my masochism*" but terrible, unbearable suffering. Though he is frequently cruel in all kinds of ways, over the past three days I have come to see how much consideration he gives me on most days. He may not stop when I say stop, but he is listening and he knows what it means in terms of my ability to last, and now I feel so helpless. I thought I was helpless before but now, with awareness of his total lack of leniency, I realise I used to have more power.

Is this reversible or is it like the price of goods? When the inflation has passed, will it go back to normal? Don't answer that.

...

I feel like a fool each time I apologise. It's not just the inherent shame of being so susceptible to a concept of right and wrong that you genuinely feel like you have to answer for it to the extent of actively suffering for your failings throughout life, it's also because, I have said it so much, the word has lost all meaning. It's the same word but when it comes from my mouth, in his direction, it may as well be empty noise. It's weightless, it's almost meaningless, does it mean anything when you are always sorry?

I am always sorry.

To him.

Only to him. In general, in life, I manage making and not making amends well, if I may say so myself, I take responsibility and I identify unnecessary blame as such, except in relationships that were traumatic and abusive. For those relationships, I am carrying around such a hefty volume of responsibility, it's as if I don't want to admit the perpetrators had a part to pay at all. That kind of helplessness, even in retrospect, is uncomfortable. I'd rather feel like I was the cause of all of it than feel like they did something to me.

...

A couple of hours after he flogged me, he came to me and bent me over the bed. He pulled my pants down to my knees and started to fuck me with a dildo. I guess what started with an overwhelming erotic itch to lay on my stomach last night is now going to be the convention. I can see the future and in it I am rolling into my stomach in dread of routine torture; I am rolling into my stomach in because this is how I must be positioned to be punished.

"You're wet," he accused me as he fucked me.

I was wet. I have been mindless with the need to be touched, dripping with the anticipation of more pain and ensorcelled by intensity of this interaction. It's been a long time since I have had the courage to be this indulgent, to be this open to the unrelenting grit of human sexuality that will go to any extent if you take me there.

"I'm sorry for being so wet," I told him, "I'm sorry for being horny."

"You should be sorry," he said, tightening his grip on the phallic appendage he wields like a machete, "It doesn't seem right for you to be so horny when you are being punished."

My mouth went dry because it was one of those things you don't want to admit to thinking, you don't want to be known to think, you don't want to hear out loud but you secretly long to be caught in a situation where you're allowed to feel it.

"Maybe you should punish me for being horny," I whispered into the quilt.

"Maybe I will," he whispered into my ear.

...

Our night together started off so friendly I almost forgot, for a moment, what we have been doing. I was occupied until ten so by the time he was able to get his hands on me too many hours had passed for him to beat me again. Or maybe that was just his benevolence. Instead I got naked and lay on my stomach, two pillows propped up under my pelvis, lifting my hips just high enough to be accessible, but not so high to be inviting. He ran his hands all over my body, all over the parts of it that he has beaten over the course of the last three days. I was so thrilled to have his hands on my body even if he wouldn't touch my cunt, I lost myself in the comfort and familiarity of this touch. For a long moment, I completely forgot to fear him and worry about what was being done to me.

Until he started to squeeze instead of rubbing.

He squeezed my aching breasts, then he squeezed the bruises on my arms, he scratched the carving on my back and started to make these sounds like he was saying he felt so much pity for me. He moved up behind me and ran his fingers over my ass. It made me shudder, I worry that his fingers and his cock interacting with my ass is also an inevitability and I don't want to think about it right now. I don't want to think about it at all. I want to live in denial right up until the moment I feel the tip of his cock against my asshole.

"If I find that you're horny, I will punish you right now," he said putting his fingers against my hole, "Every single day, I will check, whenever I want, if I find that you are horny, you'll get punished again. You should not be horny when you're in repentant disgrace, it's disgusting."

As he said the word disgusting, I felt his fingers meet the wealth of wetness aching to spill out of me. He *tutted* and then instantly began to fuck me so hard with his fingers, I started to cramp. Even as I write this, I am lying in a foetal position in the darkness because when I move the pain feels like a scream trapped inside a room, like an echo that reverberates endlessly.

"I'm sorry," I said again, but realising its hollowness followed up with, "I deserve to be punished."

I must repent so I tried to remind myself I deserve it as he fucked me, thrusting into me as if trying to shove his entire arm inside me. The moment he would stop, he would go back to touching my body, leaning into me from behind and cupping my breasts in his hands. He would squeeze and rub them until I forgot about the pain and began to moan again, lost in the trenches of arousal as if I wasn't hiding from the war, and as soon as I would begin to round the peak, he would bear down and remind me that I wasn't allowed to be aroused. He'd draw his fingers back to my cunt and pretend there was a real diagnostic procedure involved in determining whether I would be punished again or not. For a few seconds, I would fight the change in situation, begging him to see how much he was hurting me, but the self-pity disappeared quickly each time, replaced by a fervent and loyal need to prostrate myself for penance. I begged to be punished, until he stopped and went back to he rest of my body. Over and over again until I couldn't keep track of what I was supposed to be saying. Supposed to be feeling.

Finally he climbed off me and began to play with my breasts again. Slower and more gentle. His breathing deepened as my state of arousal got more and more intense.

"Are you still getting aroused?" He asked, disappointment sewn into his syllables like buttons on a well-made shirt.

"Yes master," I confessed, "I cannot help myself, I am sorry, I don't want to be horny."

"You're going to be punished for this pathetic, shameless display," he said, "Tomorrow, just know, you're going to think all of this was so sweet and gentle."

I would have apologised again, but it seemed pointless. I already knew what was going to happen. I wasn't going to stop it. Tomorrow, I will be punished again.

...

Day 4

Sometimes I wonder why I insist on living my sexuality so publicly. Outside of the writerly interest in exploring sexuality in a literary way and divorced from the general desire for validation that plagues all artists, there are more sexual reasons for why I do it. It is thrilling, for certain, to elicit a very specific response in people, a concoction of arousal and despair that hurts the brain and makes the body yearn. Over the years the accusations that the things I write are *disturbing* have stopped bothering me and encouraged me to look into *what* is disturbing and I think I get it. The things I write about are easy to *other*, as a character on the pornographic internet I don't need to be thought of as *real*, I can be seen the same way as we see porn actors who insert alarmingly large devices into their orifices or ones who appear to be living in basements for years. I can be viewed with the plausible deniability of a staged act (and of course, there is some staging, or at least, some strategic placement of information in a way that turns a conversation into dialogue but that comes from the writer, not the sexual being) when it comes to the subjects about which I write, the acts I seem to perform.

But.

I write from a very human place. I write from the place where the act becomes sentient and begins to consider its own humanity, out loud, in the middle of the performance, and I think that makes me relatable because on the emotional level we're all pretty similar in terms of what we experience, it's just the stimulus that elicits a particular emotion that differs. Even when I write about things that one may never think to do or have ever thought could be arousing, the fact that human beings will always be able to see the human being in me makes it more terrifying and disturbing. The fact that alongside the disturbia of the need for maudlin suffering and the fetishism of trauma, I can also be seen as the person who experiences the pedestrian ennui of life, the tenderness of the love of an animal, the existential dread of the human condition and a person who experiences all of the normalcy in the world makes it more scary. It's like finding out your nice-seeming neighbor who always gave you a cup of sugar and watered your plants was the serial killer. It's harder to view only the demon when you are privy to so much more information about the human. You can't help but see it as yourself or yourself as it.

I totally do it on purpose.

It's fun, outside of the fact that my sexuality is pervasive and lives in every realm, it's just fun. It's entertaining to see responses in people, it's gratifying to force sexuality into the same realm as the rest of life and remove the possibility of its extrication. I could write things that are just hot, after all no one wants to think about the *tick-tock* of the life clock when they're reading about the erotic humiliation of a big-titty hussie, but it feels dishonest to pretend those thoughts and experiences disappear in the sexual realm. It feels incomplete not to bring all of life into this space of erotic non-fiction. I want it there, I want to see what it does to people. It's for my own titillation.

But there is exhibitionism to it as well.

I want to be seen in my suffering. I don't care for the exhibition of my body, I enjoy exposure that is humiliating, but the act of flashing my ass or tits does absolutely nothing for me. I don't care if anyone thinks it is hot or beautiful. I don't want anyone to look at my body. I want you to look at my pain. I don't mean look at my bruises either, the visual exposure is a tool of business to be honest, I would never take another picture if I didn't have to use them to do the disgusting act of driving up traffic so I can redirect more of it to my writing, and wallet. Bruises don't demonstrate suffering well, it's not the right medium to evoke the specificity of human emotions that take an experience from jarring to harrowing. Harrowing is all about the details. Harrowing is about feeling sorrow for what you see in me. Harrowing is about those parts of your heart that read me and feel bad for me. Pity. Horror. Despair. Hurt.

But it's not just exhibitionism.

It's a little bit more because it's important to my pleasure of demonstration that the reader be turned on by it as well. Even, and hopefully, despite themselves. Feel sorry for me, please, but enjoy my misery as well. Get off to it. It's horrible, like finding a person passed out in the street and stealing their wallet before calling an ambulance, if you call it at all. That's what really turns me on about living my sexuality so publicly, I like that response that makes you just a little wrecthed for wanting to see what else could happen to me, for liking the horrible things that I am experiencing, for relishing them. It's not enough that I be seen in misery and evoke emotion, I want to cause the wrong emotion as well. That's the most human thing about us all, we all feel good when we should feel bad. Should is a construct. Doesn't it feel so good, to poke it?

...

The kid is home today, he has to take his final exams and he has to study more than I am comfortable with anyone having to study. I don't like this format of testing at all, but I haven't quite found a way out of this system. I also had a tonne of work to do today. My husband, the monster, spent his morning retrieving objects of genital torture from the big, steel closet where he house all the bad things. I don't think he intends to beat me today, I think all of his intentions are centered around my cunt, and building on the terrible conundrum of being aroused because you're not allowed to be aroused.

As I worked at my desk, he put a whole bunch of objects on the bed and cleaned them. Pipes, hoses, hammers. It really was a nice time, I now remember, when he was still fucking me with things like dildos and his cock, which actually are designed to be in there. He told me in the morning that he would teach me not to be turned on by my punishment or punish me for it until I died. I did die in response to that sentence, does that mean my punishment is over? After he finished he took the kid for a haircut, I went to lock the door and as we waiting for the child to pee, put on his shoes, change his shoes, comb his hair, realise he didn't have to comb his hair, pee again, he leaned over me beside the door, against the wall. He had a beard, it's gone now, but on the occasions when he is on leave, he usually shaves once every three days instead of the daily shave to which he, and I, are accustomed. I don't like the beard. I touched it. I asked him if he was going to shave and then I felt bad for imposing my expectations on his appearance. I genuinely felt bad about that. He laughed at me.

"When I come back," he started to whisper into my ear, his tone like an amused, insouciant executioner, "I'm going to punish your cunt. You're going to be so, so sorry for how you behaved last night."

I am scared. I really am scared now. I can take an alarming number of consecutive beatings. My masochistic brain is wired a specific way, more pain makes me want more pain. The first beating is hard, the ninth beating is inevitable.

But this.

This is terrifying to me. I do not understand his fixation with genital torture, I do not understand my own fixation with it either, but it's vital to our relationship. I do also understand that I cannot take it. I have a vagina that rips at three fingers. It *rips*. I cannot. I have a vagina that is naturally inclined to resisting any kind of penetration and over the years it has come to fear his the most. The fear of it has turned into nausea today. As he told me what he was going to do, I found myself wanting to vomit.

I didn't.

I just waited.

...

He came back home and shaved. I was too deep inside my work to be distracted, I think he is able to tell, mostly because, I have a very clear tell. When I am deeply immersed, I start reciting what I am typing out loud whispers, it helps me, but I forget that I am not always alone at my desk. Sometimes people can hear me, I wonder if I am coherent. I took vague note of the fact that he was moving around the house, talking to the kid, taking a shower, walking the dog. By the time I finished, he was sitting on the bed, watching True Detective. I asked him if I could get on the bed.

The furniture rule is one of those extremely arbitrary rules of which there is no even, fair enforcement. Some days, he wants me to ask. Some days, he whacks me for wasting his time by asking something that is so obviously what he needs me to do. Some days he wants me randomly thank him for the privilege of being on his bed. Some days he tosses me out of bed because I didn't ask to be in it, other days it's a complete non-issue. For a person as fixated on clarity as I am, I sure can enjoy the stochastic implementation of this rule. It's because I am comfortable with his right to make and change the rules without so much as informing me of them, especially when it comes to his belongings. I tend to think of our things, our spaces, as his. I often call it his room, his bed, his couch, his table even when legally and financially I am an equal party to them. The encumbrance of ownership is a bit much for my sensibility anyway, I fear losing no things because I own no things, that is the belief system within which I am most comfortable.

As soon as I got on the bed, he came towards me, lifting me up to my knees so he was looking right into my eyes.

"So you like to get horny when you're being punished?" He asked, pushing the hair off my face and tucking it behind my ear, "It's time to confront this bad, bad behaviour."

He gestured that I should take off my pants and while I was doing so he placed a pillow in the middle of the bed. I put them on the chair and made my way back to the bed, trembling and despondent, I crawled back into bed and got on my stomach.

"Put your face in the pillow, there's no way you are getting through this without screaming," he said, "But that still doesn't mean I want your shrieks to disturb my peace."

Where did you get this peace, my love? Was it from watching True Detective? I would never have said that out loud, but it did occur to me, and deep inside my mind, in a place where I still smile and believe in sunshine, I was amused by it. I saw his fingers, through the crack of light between the pillow and my face, as he picked up the pipes he had laid out on the bed earlier in the day. Why do we have to do this? Can he not just beat me and beat me again? It's a little hole, how much torture can it take? Please.

He put his hand on the small of my back and applied just a little bit of pressure, I lifted my hips because my body knows exactly how to respond to him even when it knows it will not enjoy whatever is coming. I would wish I wasn't so easy if there wasn't such divine pleasure to obeying him under every circumstance. Compliance is a sex-toy. They're all sex-toys, goddamn emotions, I would have nothing to do with them if they didn't turn me on so much. With his other hand he began to work the pipe into me, it's flexible enough to be doubled and tripled but rigid enough to have jagged edges. My insides were already so sore and vulnerable, but he was determined not to relent so I attempted to negotiate with myself to just suspend the reception of pain and get through it.

That never works.

I was screaming into the pillow within seconds. I can never explain exactly how this makes me feel but I always know when someone else gets it. It's an experience too vast to elucidate and too particular to mistake. Its such covert torture too, no one will ever see it inside me and no one will ever know how much violence he left inside me. I will never be able to brandish these bruises as evidence of my suffering, my word will have to be enough and it isn't. My words aren't equipped to explain this. The pain inside me is eternal, each person who has added to it, in welcome arenas of torture or terrible circumstances of my misfortune, left it in there forever. My cunt is where all the violence ever committed unto me resides. Each subsequent attack is adding to the vault, it's stepping on old wounds, it's ripping out the sutures I have so carefully reapplied after the last disturbance; it's wrecking a precarious ecosystem, a precise disruption of which could potentially bring down my entire world.

It is impossible for me not to react to penetration, even when I negotiate with myself and resolve to behave, I will usually say or do something that is not allowed. I will scream, wriggle, beg him to stop or try to get it out of me. I wish I could get raped better but I can't. I am unfixable. Incorrigible. That's why he has to do this to me. I got a little self-indulgent with the trauma-porn there, but it's true in its own sad, little way. There is an essence to suffering for your own needs that is absent in other interactions of this nature. A possibility. When he hurts me for him, he is evil, and I can get off to that, it's beautiful to see evil unleash itself upon you, but when I ask to be hurt because I am evil, because that is what I deserve, it's dirtier. Repentance is dirtier than reception. I will sign that in blood.

Blood that he will probably draw out of my cunt by fucking it with things that do not belong in there. I screamed out loud. I feel like I cannot do anything right. The amount that I have been heard in the last four days is usually how much I scream in four months. It makes me feel like such a disappointment and this emotion, the disappointment, it's like a fucking sleeper cell in this terrorist organisation that is his love. It's just a twinge of pain in my heart right now, I barely notice it because I am so occupied by the overwhelming pain in my body, but it's invading me from the inside. Days later, when my body is wasted, my heart will be ready for him to devastate, this feeling will have spread like an infection. It's surreal, I can see my own deconstruction, I can chart it, I can delineate it with academic expertise, but I can't stop it.

Nah.

I won't stop it.

It's not just the person sticking pipes inside a cunt who is dirty and sick, the cunt could be just as vile. I am. It's why I deserve this. Or at least, I'd like to pretend it's why so that I don't have to admit that all of this strange fixation on having my cunt hurt in a specific way may have been completely absent from my life if I hadn't had a few orgasms on a cock I didn't consent to having inside me inside me eighteen years ago. I'd like to believe I'm not still punishing myself for that, or worse, I'd like not to discover that I failed to forgive myself for something that was not my fault because the sexual mess I made in the aftermath of dealing with it was too much fun for me to give up. It's that one. That's the one that's the real reason why I know I deserve to be punished.

But not like this.

Or at least, when he was fucking me with the pipe, I felt that way. It's panicky. I screamed out loud because there was no place left in my body for the reflexes to be absorbed. I'll be better. I'll learn to be better.

"Put your head back fucking down in the pillow or you're about to feel my elbow on your back," he said.

Specific threats. So specific. I used to wriggle when he used to fuck me years ago, what a quaint little trip down the worst memory lane this is, like a picnic in Chernobyl, he would keep me place but putting the tip of his elbow on the small of my back. It's very effective, because the amount of pain it causes is violently disproportionate to the effort. I like receiving the message that I can be annihilated with very little work on his part. I put my face down in the pillow again. I often try to think about how it feels to just have someone obey you, no matter the circumstances, is it a rush? Is it thrilling to watch your whims and words turn into someone's behaviour? Personality? Life? Nightmare? I get to nightmare so quickly. Like a one-trick pony that's not even great at the one trick. I swear I don't hate myself, it's dirty talk. These are the only filthy words that make me wet.

Wet is what got me to the place of being fucked with pipes. He was pushing them in so deep, it felt like I would throw up all over the bed. I may have apologised, I may not have, I don't know. It's not the apology he is after anymore, either. He likes it when I thank him for punishing me. I've been doing it. I like it too. It's just so helpless and sad, makes your clit swell in the kind of pride a bad mom feels when she finds out her fourteen-year old daughter is taking diet pills. I thanked him and he rewarded me by fucking me harder, I respect it, he has to keep me guessing, if he softened each time I behave well, I would have no choice but to use it to try to manipulate him. He'd understand that too, he'd punish me for it, but he'd understand. Twenty minutes into fucking me, and it was twenty minutes because I keep excellent track of time because I am a schedule-neurotic, he took out the pipes and replaced them with his fingers. I could no longer tell if one was better than the other, I just wanted it to stop.

I started begging and promising to never be wet again. To never even think about being turned on again. I started to apologise like a chant of amends, begging to be heard, I just needed him to know.

"Will you get horny again when you are being punished?" He asked.

"I won't, I promise," I lied.

Though, not in the moment. In the moment I really wasn't horny, not even wet, it was drier inside me than the air in this city.

"Let me check that," he said, pulling out of me, "Get on your back."

I got on my back and he pulled by breasts out of my tank top, the moment I realised what he was intending to do, I felt the overwhelming urge to beg him not to do it.

"I just punished you for being horny in a state of penance," he started, rubbing my breasts and squeezing them just a little bit, not enough to hurt, only enough to arouse, "You shouldn't get horny immediately after if you have learnt your lesson. You won't, right?"

I begged and begged like a broken record that wasn't even playing a good song to start with, I begged because I was instantly turned on, and I wasn't going to be able to hide it.

"Spread your legs, let me see," he asked, using the honeyed voice he uses to declare my doom to me.

That voice makes me so wet and ashamed. He didn't touch my cunt but I could feel his gaze on it as his hands continued to play with my breasts. I think I have transferred all my sexual energy to them because I am giving up his touch on my cunt. It's the only place where he will still touch me to turn me on like a person. I tried to fight the arousal, I tried to fight it like an orgasm you aren't allowed to have but I could feel it growing between my legs.

"Oh my god," he said, half-laughing in distillation of cruelty to a tone of voice, "I can see your clit getting swollen."

He stopped touching my breasts and moved off the bed. He stood between my legs and with a single finger poked at my hole, he swiped at the wetness and rubbed it off on my thigh.

"Wet, again," he growled, "Do you never tire of disappointing me?"

I do. I tire of it but I don't know how to do better. I didn't say anything. I waited for the sentence I knew was coming.

"We're just going to have to try to teach you this lesson harder tonight," he said walking away, "Put your pants back on now, disappointment."

"I'm sorry master," I said, as I stepped off the bed to reach for my pants, "Thank you for punishing me."

I wonder if I should keep count of how many times I have already said that.

...

He put me in the corner. He made me scream, cry and beg until I lost control of my words and then he put me in the corner. He pushed my face into it and left me there. I wanted to be there. I have been wanting to be there all day. It's not a place to hide. It's not just a place to hide, anyway. From across the room he dared me to get wet again, he dared me to show him the needs of my body again, he dared me to be a pathetic, ingrate again.

I hate that every word he said turned me on.

I cannot be fixed. This cannot be fixed. He will keep punishing me for being a human being and I won't be able to stop. I'm sorry, please, I am sorry.

I wish I could be less.

I wish I could be less than human.

Leave me in the corner, until I am.

...

Day 5

I had a little bit of a breakdown last night. He said he saw it coming a mile away but I didn't see it coming at all. I wonder if I should believe him. I cried a great deal, and oscillated between intense sexual arousal and terrible emotional turmoil. I realise that sounds exactly the same as my constant state of being these days, but it was different. I asked him if he still loved me. Why would I ask him that? It's so embarrassing to have emotions out loud, like taking a piss in public, in the middle of the town square, into a bucket placed between your feet, while everyone watches.

I once read some erotica about something really similar. It was about a woman who had been sentenced to public humiliation by a court of some kind of law in an alternate world order. It may have been a futuristic dystopia of some kind but the punishment for the iniquity of women had the flavor of medieval times, a lot of times the depiction of the future in pop culture feels like it is informed too heavily by the past. I understand it a little bit, if we could write the future, wouldn't we be able to predict it more accurately as well? In the story, this woman was to stand naked on a stage in the town square, her hands tied up and her legs, there was be a bucket in the middle of her legs but she could only pee a little at a time, there was a specified amount and the bucket was marked. There was a mandatory amount of water she had to consume over the course of the hours she would be there, but she could only expel a certain quantity. It was very specific. It made me uncomfortable, but it also taught me that good writing is entirely about specificity. You dig, dig, dig until you get to a place of exactness. Exactness is evocative. Exactness hurts like a scalpel, the pain is granular, it's deep. You can locate it with complete accuracy.

Emotional exposition feels like that because I know in explicit detail exactly what was driving the vulnerability that made me ask him if he still loves me.

"So am I going to have a breakdown every four days, you think?" I asked him after my tears had been contained by his tenderness.

"Probably," he said, "It could be more often."

It could, couldn't it? Really, what am I doing? This imposition of supplicant remorse and overwhelming physical experience that I have placed on myself in the name of an erotic exploration of the soul is so wild and untamed. My body is easy, it will take what it is given, but my heart is cracking. Even when you know in your bones that you are loved, such cruelty is so hard to accept as a temporary condition. It's like Sirius, our dog, whenever we leave the house without her, she doesn't ever believe that we will come back. I am worried my heart won't ever return from this trip. Yet I want to take it, because strife is so alluring. And strife in this form, it feels more meaningful, even though it isn't, nothing is. I've been reading The Myth of Sisyphus by Albert Camus (and I wish more polemics were written in our time), and I find some truth in the idea that the acceptance of the meaninglessness of all of life is a mindspace that is dangerous to individuals when contemplating whether one should live or not. I refrain from discussing this subject out loud around too many people because it's so fraught, perhaps as it should be, but it's one I think about a lot.

Of late I am so bothered by the people in the world. I have reached the place where I find it unbearable to have to parse through the words of people to find their intentions. I am told my expectations of honesty are unreasonable, and maybe they are, but dishonesty when it is directed at me feels like an attack, and because my emotional structure is how it is, I can never tell I am being attacked. I just feel, uncomfortable. I feel unable to form new relationships with people, I feel unable to commit to old ones in the same way, I would talk about it with everyone, but people don't talk truthfully. They make excuses and they build tales, and these words feel like acid being poured into my ears. I also feel watched and studied, not just by the people in my life, but also by the people I don't know are in my life. I was deeply impacted by being plagiarized last year and I have since discovered that it wasn't a single incident by a single person, it was happening in a pattern, people don't just steal exact sentences and words, they steal ideas and identities, they pose as me sometimes. There is a type of identity theft that isn't about papers and credit cards, but about essence. I didn't think I would ever care about, or even notice, something like that but I care and I notice, and it makes me wonder about myself. Why do I believe I own a patent to myself? To my work even? There is nothing special to me, why does it matter if my inane generic nature was robbed? For a person so allegedly committed to detachment, why do I care?

I've always let people take from me, anything they want, they can have a jacket, my earrings or an idea I may have had, I give it freely, but perhaps it is the fact that I wasn't asked, I was taken. I am attempting to recover from these feelings of alienation from the world but I worry that this was always the eventual destination for me. I am no longer able to show myself, really share myself, with the people who are actually, physically in my life (well, except him, and the kid) and it's not because they aren't interested or there, it's because I know I will not be understood. It's not a matter of intelligence or interest, maybe it's a matter of insanity, but I feel like the only person in a town who doesn't speak the local language. I am not sure what that has to do with the numinous suffering I undertake, but maybe it's just to demonstrate that this is what I would rather do with my time. It's tumultuous, but at least when it comes to my intentions for myself, I know them.

...

I kept the tip of the cane after it broke off while he was caning my thighs in the afternoon. He gave it to me, I am certain he didn't mean to make a present of it, but as soon as he handed it to me it acquired some value that made me want to hold on to it. I held it to my chest and I went to use the toilet, and then I put it in my drawer. Maybe I would like to imbibe it with my blood, or my tears. I don't know for sure what I would like to do with it, but there is something, it will reveal itself in time, but I do wonder why I hung onto it in such a furtive manner. As if revealing to him that I did would get me in trouble.

I think I am adjusting to the harsh nature of the beatings he is delivering to me these days, I was very calm while he caned me. He was very quiet. I was talking to myself about the need to react, not out loud, but emotionally and within myself, to every single blow. Sometimes, it gets a little bit pedantic, when I internally ask questions like — Why did you hit me there twice in a row? Why didn't you switch sides in keeping with the pattern? Why did you hit me so much harder than the last blow? These questions, usually come up in the first ten minutes of being hurt, before one slips into the space of silence that is evoked only by pain, but even in those ten minutes it is clear how they are borne from a need to wrestle for control. Either someone else is allowed to do to you as they please or they aren't. Either you are available to be impacted by the influence of another, or you're not. If I am, these questions are futile. I would like to erode this need to question, even internally, in the interest of a conceptual idea of freedom that could be real.

Would the pain feel any different if I didn't try to structure it in my head?

In the morning, right after we woke up, he fucked me. It was a kindness. I needed him inside me, I needed to feel his pleasure in me, as cold and dispassionate as his rituals of love-making are as they pertain to me, they are a semblance of normalcy. They're the intimacy that I understand. I think my cunt is swollen shut now, I am only exaggerating slightly, but I don't feel as helplessly horny as I did until yesterday. I feel determined, not to behave in a certain way, but to delve past the simplistic pleasure and pain of genital reactions. Today feels very internal, the voices inside me are louder than the world, and there is comfort in this retreat. I am fielding bigger questions, issues that are more uncomfortable. I wonder if it appears as if my sexuality is my means to introspection, it probably does, but it's not so linear. The intense immersion in a sexual construct allows me the space to delve completely into the effort to write it, I am alone in the lab with my microscope, and there are so many samples that have been unearthed by this persistent state of emotionality that I am consumed. I aimed to overwhelm myself and now I have, this state is what spurs me to write with such determined focus. It's the writing that allows me to introspect, the sexuality is the narrative within which I am conducting my research. It creates the dire straits I need to engage the most of me.

Is that a little weird? Well, then it's a little weird. Perhaps it is time to stop aspiring to the normalcy that I have insisted is the most vital part of me because I want to make sense of my life. I want to look back at it and be able to say: *Oh it's just the usual stuff, it's like everybody's life.* There is a comfort to being included in the covenant of normal, especially for those of us who grew up and lived with life experiences that may have been somewhat harrowing. I just want everyone to know that I am perfectly functional as an adult and that there has been nothing in my life that is any different from anyone else's because any deviation from that means I must confront the abnormality of the circumstances in which I was born, raised, lived and hurt.

Perhaps it is time to stop fighting the strangeness.

Maybe I'm a little weird.

So what?

...

Ever since he has been off work and at home, I've pulled the armchair in our room to the front of my desk for him to sit at when I am taking a break from work but I'm not done working. A couple of days ago, I sensed that he may eventually experience, or may have already experienced, some emotional discomfort from enforcing the condition of continuous unrelenting excessive cruelty so, as a joke, I asked him to step into my office for a debriefing. The joke turned into an excellent and vital conversation about managing the expectations of one another and balancing them against our own needs and excesses. It created a space for us to step outside of the construct and communicate.

Today, I needed to be debriefed.

I'm fine. I am. I am just confronting something about myself that I have avoided for a long time; I am contemplating the validity of all the guilt that I have carried around my entire life. The fact that I am so committed to the suspension of disbelief around this endeavour, allowing myself to *know* and accept that everything I have ever done wrong, I am being punished for it now, I am paying for it, in a manner that I understand, has also allowed me to actually consider the source of all the guilt. To think about it without panic. To wonder if it is warranted. The act of direct suffering has made me see the possibility of exoneration, but more importantly, the futility of the standards to which I hold myself. The harshness of the expectations to which I have subjected myself.

I cried while I talked about it with him.

In my office.

It wasn't the kind of crying to which I am accustomed, I try to keep all of my expression of pain and emotion restricted to a sexual or artful realm, no need for it to get too personal, you know, but this wasn't sexual. It was therapist-crying. It was the kind of crying you do when you finally allow yourself to be a human being for a minute and admit that you've been a tad hard on yourself. I'm realising that I straddle this line between the insanity allowed to artists and the extreme functionality expected from professionals, and in straddling it, I have lost some of my madness. I used to live a lot more intuitively. I worried less about being perfect but I have something in invested in proving, to the odds more than anything else, that people like me can turn out okay. That people like me, with all the rape and childhood abuse and domestic abuse and more rape and eating disorders and PTSD, can be perfectly functional. Just, perfect. Never miss a deadline. Always have a homemade cake in the fridge. Consistently there for my kid. Helping the entire community with everything. There when you need someone for support in the middle of the night. On top of what everyone needs.

Fighting for everyone's rights. Caring for all the animals. Always achieving, never asking to be noted for it. I have to be perfect or the statistics win.

But seriously, am I really going to battle..statistics? Statistics do not give a shit about me. No one does, really, and I mean that in the least nihilistic way I have ever meant it. For whom, am I trying to be so perfect? For what? The artist demands something else from me, something that has always made me live my life more joyfully, it demands that I commit to my whims and my constructs, to my ideas and my creativity, to notions of erotic Lent, or weeks spent in communal hotbeds trying to find the version of God that's causing all the trouble and accidentally creating all this beauty. The artist has always demanded that I do what occurs intuitively, go where I think I need to go to create, put myself in whatever state I need to in order to be able to enable the exact realm of experience from which I wish to create. If that meant I should be a sex worker, I did it, because the artist demanded it. If that meant I should commit to being locked up in a basement, I did it, because the artist needed access to that voice. If that meant I should wake up and decide I needed to move to a different city the next day, I did it, because the artist needed to write there. I make concessions for the artist, because all of my joy is there. All of it. The artist is not afraid of pain. The artist is not afraid of life.

But this? Little Miss Perfect? She's afraid. Even when it comes to pain she wants to curate, manage, organise. When it comes to all of life, she wants to schedule. She wants to discipline the creativity and don't get me wrong, I appreciate some of this. Discipline is exactly what most creatives lack, it's what keeps the world from hearing their voices. Most writers spend 80% of their time thinking of writing, 10% of it planning to write and 10% of it writing. Little Miss Perfect gave me the habits that ensure I spend 80% of my time writing, and both professionally and artistically, I have benefitted from that discipline. But, I may also have over-corrected and quashed some of my own freedom. The artist must have its madness, for soon enough, without it, it shall lose the curiosity and wonder that drives creation.

I have to give myself back the madness.

I have to cut off the infected leg.

Because what will happen, really? What will happen if I don't micromanage or try to micromanage every aspect of every part of the world that crosses my path every single day? If I don't make myself responsible for everyone's problems? If I don't file twenty petitions a week? If I try to exist in spaces without ensuring that I am always a non-issue? I want to exist in the lives of people without the right to have an impact, I dread the possibility that I could negatively impact someone. Who the fuck am I trying to be?

And why?

I am denying myself the most vital element of myself. The courage to live in all of life's extremities and insanities. The fearlessness with which I can approach situations because it matters less that I be comfortable, than I be privy to the state of existence, the entire life-experience that awaits me, when I allow myself to prioritise creation and discovery. From whom am I trying to earn this tag of normalcy? Just to be able to say that everything that happened in my life happens to everyone so I can keep feeling like I am okay?

I cried because I finally said it out loud. It wasn't okay. My life wasn't "normal." I will not fix it by forcing myself into social conventions that stamp me as upstanding, contributory and productive. You cannot fix the past. I do not wish to try anymore. What would happen if I gave myself permission to be free? Is it insane that I want to do things — strange things, unusual things, difficult things, unprecedented things, intense things, things that cause debilitating change and unprecedented trauma — primarily because I want to joy of writing them? Yes, it is.

Why should I let that stop me?

Because people will think I am crazy?

The thing is, they already do.

...

I felt an emotional lassitude after I returned home from the gym, I thought my heart was fatigued, but there was something I had been wanting to do all day. I went to the gym early, I rushed through my workout, because I wanted to come back home and polish all of his shoes. I wanted to buff and shine until my shoulders hurt. Until I could see the sparkle in the leather. I took them all out from the rack and placed them on the floor, I brought the polish and the brush. He watched me, silently bemused, for a while.

"What are you doing?" He asked, finally.

"I want to polish all of your shoes," I responded, because I could not, at the time, offer the essay-version of the answer.

"I'm not going to work though," he said, still unable to assess the situation, "Why are you polishing all my shoes?"

"I have to," I told him, "Please, may I?"

He nodded his head. I sat on the floor, resting my elbows on the stripes of the cane on my thighs from this afternoon, and one by one, I began to polish his shoes. I did the brogues first. He doesn't wear them very often, only with one set of uniforms, and he doesn't have to wear that uniform very often. Tending to shoes is not about leather for me at all. I don't find leather sexy, I don't think it is cool, I don't find it beautiful, I don't even know enough about the history or ritualistic maintenance protocols of leather. This is about shoes. Tending to his shoes means polishing them, tending to the shoes of another may mean something else. There is something religious about this for me even though I am not a religious person. The thing I like most about the religion of my father (which is Sikhism) is that prayer in the form of service is the most admissible and encouraged form of worship. Especially service that humbles you. So, at the Gurudwara, every person, is encouraged to serve the community through invisible, quiet acts of service. Serve food, wash the dishes, cut the vegetables for the food service, wash the kitchen floors. It's all necessary physical labour. You are just allowed to find work for yourself, expected even, they leave it out for the community to do, but you don't assert yourself to be recognised in your service at all. If ever anyone asks, "*Who cooked this food?*" you never answer with your own name, even if it was you. There is no social goodwill. And because prayer of this kind is so normalised where we used to live (because of the majority religion being Sikhism), you are no better than anyone else for doing it.

The children were encouraged to do the shoe-service which is to organise, arrange and return people's shoes after they were done with prayers. I never used to go inside the temple because I've had an *opinion* on religion and God for a long time, but I loved doing the shoe service. I don't know why it is humbling to tend to people's shoes, it's possibly because of the least imaginative association with feet being the lowest of a person, but I still find it humbling. I will always do whatever a lover needs for their shoes.

He needed me to polish them.

Well, he didn't, when we first met, he was appalled at the idea that I polish his shoes. A month into dating, the morning after he had just beaten and fucked me for the first time (which, I still cannot believe he made me wait a month nor that I enjoyed it), it was Sunday, he pulled his shoes out and said he was going to polish them. I just had to do it. I asked immediately. I told him, immediately, that I would do it for the rest of my life. I know that's a bit much for a month of being together, but you had to be there, you would have seen we were already entrenched in forever. He was hesitant, the soldier's trepidation to let another do this kind of work is something I now understand, the cultural hypocrisy of families teaching men not to have women tend to their feet despite how women are treated in this country, is something I still do not understand, but neither reason was sufficient for me. I begged him to let me do it. He relented.

I did it wrong.

Actually, I had never polished a shoe before in my life. I'm dirty shoes and unironed shirts. That's who I am. There was never cause for me to polish my shoes nor those of anyone else so I thought all you have to do is coat it in a thick layer of polish and it's done. I liked it too, the matte-finish of the shoes, and I showed him with pride.

"But you didn't..you didn't polish them, my love?" He said, trying to be as gentle as possible.

"What do you mean?" I asked, "I did!"

"Do you...not know how to polish shoes?" He asked me, putting his arm around me.

I felt like a fool. Like an idiotic little girl playing with her mother's pearls.

"I will teach you," he said, taking the shoe from me.

He taught me. It didn't take very long, it's not a terrifyingly complex process. He showed me on one shoe, made me practice the process and then he handed me the other shoe.

"Now do it properly or I will punish you," he told me.

He punished me. He punished me every single time I polished his shoes for the next year, I really thought I just couldn't, I wouldn't ever be able to do it well enough. His evaluation was so exacting, always looking for the smallest flaw and finding it, but then after that year, he never punished me again for doing it wrong. He says I never do it wrong. I wouldn't dare.

I guess I wouldn't.

As I sat there polishing his shoes, I lost myself in them completely. I polished each shoe for much longer than it needed it. When I finished the brogues, I did the DMS. They are so heavy for shoes I could probably use them as weights in a pinch. I sat them over my aching thighs and polished them with my aching shoulders. Finally, I did his combat boots. The ones with which he beat me so brutally ereyesterday. I couldn't stop polishing them. They needed the least work, because I had just done them so recently, but I wanted to spend all my heart on them. I didn't even notice him get up and walk over to where I was sitting on the floor.

"You've been polishing that shoe for a long time," he said to me, making me jump.

"Oh," I said, my manner so cloddish the boot stumbled in my lap, "I guess I..."

"Got lost in it?" He finished for me.

"Yeah," I responded, gulping, as if I couldn't augur the situation.

"It's okay," he said, bending to stroke my cheek, "I found you."

I was about to tell him that I love him, but he cut me off, and grabbed my hand.

"As much as I love to see you bleed, the polish on your fingers is still my favourite thing to see," he said.

Should that have hurt?

It didn't.

I'm sorry I cannot suffer in service of you.

...

Day 6

He said he had to punish me for begging him to touch my cunt. I did do that. I am ashamed that I did. It was two nights ago, I was completely beside myself in need, I cannot even bring myself to repeat the things I said in the heat of the moment before devolving into an emotional mess of a human being. Yesterday, he was kinder to me, as a result of the breaking I am sure, he only beat me once, he only fucked me once and he didn't shove anything inside my cunt at all. That's the nicest he has been in days.

But, today is a different day.

He came up behind me as I lounged around the bed enjoying my Saturday morning. Saturdays make me want to go to a farmer's market, buy fresh flowers and bake a cake. I'm willing to settle for a juice shop, flowers I pick from the gardens of others and potatoes au gratin. Saturday made him lift me up by the hair, force my clothes off my body and shove his fingers back inside me. It will be something about this systematic raping that takes me down. I know it. Years ago, a decade ago, my former partner and I devised a sexual experiment in which he locked me in the basement of my grandparents old home (they were not there at the time) in the mountains for a week without my phone, clothes or really, anything. I am not even sure I could survive that now. I have no idea how I did. I read the things I wrote about it, in the aftermath, and then again, a while later, and I am horrified. Still, you'd think it would have been the controlled water supply, the strange toileting conditions, the lack of sunlight, the complete confiscation of recreation that broke me, but it was the systematic raping. I left some of my sanity in that basement. In that case it was my ass he was raping, but a hole with a history, is a hole with a history, right? I wonder if I'm on the precipice of losing some of my sanity now.

He kept pulling my hair, shaking my head from side-to-side as he fucked me with his fingers. It's so awful, even the areas outside my cunt, the parts of my ass against which his knuckles punch when he fingers it, are swollen and hurting. The more I scream and cry, the more firmly he holds me down. The more I cry, the more determined he seems to me. Even in our permanent agreement of "*I'll say stop if I need to, but you do you boo*," I rarely ever say *stop* very often. Now, I feel like I am saying it ten times a day. I wonder if I am unlearning some of the composure and silence he taught me over the past eight years, I cannot last the brutality without crumbling. (Eight years? That's almost as many years as the last one. I don't know why I would say that.) He didn't fuck me for very long, but before he left, he did shove a dildo inside me, telling me to keep it there until he returned.

He had to see a patient and take a stray puppy to the vet.

I know.

He is alarmingly human for a monster. He takes stray puppies to the vet, he has long conversations with our cats, he makes declarations of his love for Sirius at random and ad nauseum, he conspires with the child to design pranks to play on me, he cooks me an elaborate meal to celebrate a victory, he gets sleepy in under three-seconds when his head hits the pillow, he likes when I scratch his bald head, he scolds children in the street for not wearing helmets while riding their bikes, he gets sentimental about his youth when he listens to classic rock, he giggles like a goofy teenager when he is high. He is so human, but in my words, maybe that is less visible than it ought to be. His cruelty features in my writing, his tenderness does as well, but his humanity is perhaps most absent. His dichotomy is like a potent elixir, I cannot figure out how these extremes reside inside him, and how all of these hues feel completely like him. He left for a couple of hours and I kept wondering why it felt weird to exist with a cunt filled with vitrified pain.

...

He beat me and then he told me it was going to rain. He was disappointed I wasn't more grateful for the fact that he only caned my thighs once yesterday, so he caned them again, even before the stripes from yesterday could turn into the bruises of today. I'm uncomfortable with how determined he is to not feel sorry for me. In some parts of the beating, I could see him swing the cane with such force he had to have known I couldn't just lie there and be quiet. Still, he was so irascible about the noise coming from my mouth. I was barely making any noise.

I'm stuck.

I am really stuck in a place where I can do no right, and I imagine, the inevitable next step would be to divorce my gratification from right or wrong, and place it firmly in just *being* but there is still hope, or something, that shows up when he is explicitly being so harsh that it would be reasonable to expect a reaction from the recipient, and a small amount of disappointment, in response to the complete lack of leniency in face of extenuating circumstances. He's like the parent who makes you do arithmetic the day after your last exam and beats you because you put the date down wrong on the page of perfect answers. He's being my mom. I'm not touching that with a ten-foot pole, which I am sure he would try to fuck me with if he could have access to one.

I kept resolving not to beg him to stop and I kept begging him to stop. Are penitents allowed to feel like they're being tortured more for their venial sins than they deserve or is feeling that a sin in itself? I guess I will find out. The changed nature of his sadism in this period is forcing a change in my behaviour, it's forcing me to fall victim to reflex again and again. I wonder what is the real difference, it's not just the lack of consideration or adherence to established process, the fact that every caning feels like a cold-caning is secondary to..something. I guess, maybe, it's possible he is not acting purely out of sadism but a need to destroy something about me. He not even trying to make me last longer during beatings and I am not even trying to compose myself for them. Well, I am trying, I am just failing constantly.

I definitely failed this afternoon.

He told me he would do if again before we went to bed because I hadn't lasted until the cane broke. I wonder if I should just grab it and break it myself, I had that thought while he was hitting me, and then I felt a wave of shame wash over my body and leak out of my cunt.

"Every single day you disappoint me," he told me before he flung the cane beside me.

"I'm sorry," I told him, "Thank you for punishing me."

"It's about to rain, by the way," he said.

I sprang from the bed and ran to the window. I forgot my tears and my pain completely, within seconds, I was smiling so broadly, my jaw hurt from the joy. He laughed at me, but it was amicable laughter. He understands. It hasn't rained in months! I wake up wishing for rain every single day. I associate trite, over-the-top meaning to rain, I base my decision to move to entire cities on whether it rained the day I first visited. I feel welcomed when it rains for my arrival. The month we moved here? Rained all month. Record-breaking rain for the area. The year I moved to the desert, it *rained so much the streets flooded*. Rained the day I was born, it rained the day I was raped, it rained the day I met my husband, it rained that entire month. I will always, irrationally and against all admissible reason, believe that it rains for me, but I don't get to choose when that happens. It is mine to wish every single day, it is its to decide when I deserve it. It knows best. The rain knew, even, not to come down at my wedding, because I didn't care for it. I don't want to associate meaning to a party celebrating my parents' need to feed a bunch of people too much food, nor really a document I signed in the presence of a judge.

I recently found out that people in liberal communities, especially kinky and polyamorous communities, will deliberately hide that they are married. No, not in the usual way, not so that they can individually date and lie to their spouse. Collectively, couples or individuals who are married will mask the fact that they are married and say they are living together or nesting partners. I don't understand why, but the person who told me explained that in certain liberal dating circles being married is frowned-upon as being less woke or cool. This world sounds insane to me. People marry, even liberal woke people, because societal and legal systems incentivize marriage and penalize legal singlehood. Do you need to marry to procreate? No. Does it make your life easier? Yeah, sadly, it does. From inheritance to guardianship rights to school admissions, everything is easier if you are parenting in society as a married couple. It's that way about so much — health, money, taxes, income — being married, at some point, becomes a loophole you're trapped into whether you like it or not, at some unfair penalty, but doing it and pretending not to have done it doesn't fix anything at all?

I frequently talk about the fact that I got married because of my husband's job, not only because I couldn't live with him in conflict zones unless I was his wife, but also because I cannot access his healthcare unless I am a wife and while I can make the decision to pay for my own healthcare, and sometimes do, that was a good incentive for me. Do I wish for systems to be less marriage-obligate? Absolutely, but hiding that I am married won't make it so, talking about *how* my decision to marry was influenced by systemic bias is a much better place to start, in my opinion.

You'd think people would worry more about dismantling systems than seeking *woke.*

...

We were sitting together, across from each other, at the dining table. There was a man repairing the air-conditioning inside our bedroom. I was in the middle of discussing how the evolving social mores and laws about marijuana and psychedelics meant there would eventually be an overall overhaul on the generally-accepted version of the drug talk that parents gave to their children, or so I hope anyway. Instead of listening to me, he was looking at me. He was looking at my neck, and I could feel his hands around it, even though the image was being conjured in his head. He was threatening me with his eyes and it addled me. I stopped talking mid-sentence and forgot what I was saying. My mouth went dry. A little moan escaped my throat. My entire body started to tingle and melt into the chair. I feel like this a lot these days. Yesterday I told him I feel like I am constantly on the verge of tears, or greatness. Today, I feel like at any given time I want to curl up on the floor and hug my knees. I could feel his cock pulsate inside his pants, under the table when I said that sentence. I never thought I would ever meet a person who was as turned on by my misery as I am.

But this is the place I want to be.

It's about incident versus reality. Incident-based pain, like a beating and a fucking, delivered over the course of an evening is great, but suffering as a lifestyle hits different. It's world-building, much like you do when you are writing, and the best world-building takes places when you expose all of yourself. All of your shameful inner workings around arousal, the little things, like the sick pleasure of having your panties pulled down to your ankles and left there, like the particular poison of shifting around just a little bit until you're told to stay in place. The whole world lies in the little things. In the look with which he demonstrates my entire situation to me without raising a finger or an eyebrow and how it leaves me debilitated. I wonder how much we contribute to creating our monsters. He wouldn't be the same, if he hadn't been haunting me for the past eight years, if the structure he was haunting was different, he would be different.

How much of this monster did I build?

...

I fell asleep with my head against his chest on the couch in the late afternoon. I was leaning against him with my back and he was holding me, it was cool because of the rain and I was warm inside the blanket, and I just fell asleep. It's not customary for me to sleep without a two-hour ritual of convincing myself to sleep and trying to distract myself through any means necessary. I'm like a toddler when it comes to sleep. I had a dirty dream while I was asleep on him. Well, is it a dream if its just a recapitulation of what has happened earlier in the day? He was fucking me with the glass dildo and I was begging him to stop. He kept telling me he would stop as soon as I stopped getting wet so I started pleading with my cunt to not be wet anyway.

I woke up moaning.

He was watching me. When I tilted my head my back slightly, I could see the bottom half of his face, but I didn't need to see any of it to know of the disapproval. His hands moved to my breasts and he started to squeeze them just a little. I really, really do not know what has happened to my body to make my breasts act erogenous but I am actively fantasising about the way he has been touching them. Gentle and tantalizing. Soft. Like he is touching my clit. I am sure my cunt has referred itself to my breasts because it is trying to accept that it will not be touched. Yet, now, when he touches my breasts a dread starts to dawn on me, I start to cry out like a pathetic creature willing its own body to have mercy.

Still I lifted my shirt so I could feel his hands on my skin. He touched them. He held him in his hands and squeezed, repeatedly. I started to moan so loudly. I started to spread my legs and buck against the air.

"Oh no," he said, with ersatz woe and genuine pity in his tone, "It's happening again, isn't it?"

I hate when he uses this tone. I cannot describe it. It is the kind of tone villains use in movies when they tell the protagonist they are going to murder their family and make them watch. It's the tone of evil and it makes me so wet. I started to apologise, but my body was bucking and thrashing around wildly, invalidating every word of apology.

"You're getting horny again," he said, "How can you never learn? How many times will have to teach the same lesson?"

I appreciate that he keeps up the casuistry. It's colourful and entertaining, but we all know, I am never going to learn.

I can't.

Why cant I stop?

...

Did you know that love could feel bleak?

Whatever it was, the place where I was trying to get tonight, I couldn't get there. It felt like being on a train that is stalled indefinitely just two minutes away from its destination.

Two minutes from enjoying the pain.

Two minutes from hating it.

Two minutes from being able to accept it.

Two minutes from arousal.

Two minutes from peace.

I was stuck, two minutes away, from myself.

I seen unable to do anything right and I am sure, now, that it is by design. The point of Lent isn't to be perfect right? It's to try to circumvent your pleasure, correct your flaws and to fail so you can keep swimming in the guilt. I feel like I am failing constantly. Earlier tonight he called me a terrible slave. I *know* he doesn't *really* mean that, but I also know, that he does. In whatever reality he does say it, he means it. He wants me to know I cannot do anything right and I cannot. I cannot be beaten right. I cannot be fucked right. I cannot be tortured right. I cannot even cry right. I want to slap myself, I felt the overwhelming urge to do it as I lay in bed beside him, after he finished demonstrating to me, yet again, that I will get aroused and show it, no matter how much he punishes my cunt. I know this test is rigged, I know, but I can't help but find the inadequacy in myself. I know this game favours the house but I can't help but hope that I will have a win. If I erase everything human about me, will I finally stop being bad?

Will I finally be fixed?

Probably not.

I can't do anything right.

...

Day 7

I am struggling. It's not really because of the physical assault, it's more about the ability to continue to focus on this endeavour with such intensity while still existing in the world. It's a little bit difficult. The rest of the world continues to exist and I'd like to pause it all for just a little while. I'd like to pause the e-mails in which I have to pretend that I care about semantics, budgets and politesse. I'd like to pause the need to eat and drink to be able to continue living. I'd like to pause the interactions that people feel comfortable having with me because I am a human being who exists in the social sphere. I am unable to summon the ability to care about these things. Last night, a friend of mine called to ask me if I wanted to join her at a women's day walkathon (hosted by an "NGO" that services the army, with which I have a huge socio political problem and about whom I wrote a series of exposés that got me the most hate, and the most support, for any work I have ever done in my life). I told her I did not wish to go because of who was hosting the event, she asked why, I told her it was a matter of principle. That was as far as I could have communicated. She kept pressing for more information, like I had to make a case for declining an invitation to an event.

Most days, I would be happy to explain the politics that keep me from participating, but I was so tired by the conversation the moment I saw my phone ring. I want everyone, but him, to forget that I exist for another week. See, that was the benefit of the basement, I really was removed from the world. This is a different kind of prison, the kind I am constantly carrying with me but my shackles are invisible, I cannot explain to the world that I am carrying out a sentence. I'm doing two weeks of hard time and I cannot pretend to care about the explanation someone needs for my principles enough to provide it. That world feels alien to me right now. As the days go by, every single interruption, from phone calls to dinner to having to stand on my feet, feels like an interruption that is harder and harder to bear. I'd much rather be chained up and unable to communicate. I am so reactive to the disruption. I was genuinely annoyed by this phone call, I felt the annoyance in my body, my head hurt when I had to put dinner together and more when I had to feed myself, I am even finding it harder to be at the gym, not because I don't want to workout but because there are too many people around me, pretending the world is just a normal place, and I don't want to be reminded of that. The pedestrian is grating. The diurnal routine feels like an affront. Mundanity feels like a bird chirping right outside my window at 5 AM. I wish the sun would stop rising.

I am more reactive to the world than I have ever been before, it's as if my emotional range expanded overnight, instead of feeling only good, bad and horny (which is a mix of good and bad), I am feeling *everything*. Perhaps that is the challenge on which I should focus, how does one remain inside oneself when the world insists on continuing to be a sonorous echo of itself? I used to think the only way to do that was to make your insides louder than the outside, but it isn't working.

I wonder, maybe, if it's time to allow myself silence.

...

I barely reacted at all when he fucked me this morning. It felt like tragedy. I could see myself, lifeless and resigned, woefully draped over the bed like the bloodied saree of a martyr, but there was no fight in me at all. That did not make it easier to bear, I really think either he needs to stop hurting my cunt for a bit or we are about to find out how traumatic gynaecological emergencies are dealt with in this state. I want that to be hyperbolic, but I vacillate on whether it really is.

The brokenness is welcome though.

I can feel it in my eyes. I can feel my resignation taking over my body and mind. There is nothing I can do. In the first days, I was excited but unsure I could actually do this, in the couple that followed, I was feisty and determined, in the couple after that I was resolved and scared, but now I am just broken. There is no way out. I am in the middle of the maze and I have to do as much work to go back as I have to do to finish. It's Wednesday. It's the curse of the middle. There is no place better to go. I am stuck in a series of Wednesdays. This is the nightmare I should have seen coming.

Where you gonna run now?

...

There was an upside-down teddy bear drying on a table in my neighbor's yard. The first time I saw it, three days ago, I felt like it. I felt like a cherished object left in an intermittent state imitating discard while it recovered from its cleansing. Yesterday, I feel envious of it. It was forgotten, in the way that things can only be forgotten when you know exactly where they are, I wanted to be forgotten like that. If he forgot me, he wouldn't hurt me anymore. It's gone now. It has been inevitably remembered and brought back to its place. I long for other states, but that is where I'd like most to be. It's not terrifying anymore. I am not afraid anymore.

In the early afternoon, he was sitting on the bed and I was on my bench, we were talking, as we do every single day of our lives, I was telling him that I no longer feel the sense of dread with which I have been living for the past few days.

"It will be back, you're only halfway through your penance," he said, smiling at me with half his mouth, "It's easy to not be afraid of the dark in the afternoon."

"I'm afraid of the afternoon," I told him.

I am unable to communicate what it is I feel. It's one of those emotions that can only be demonstrated by action and lust. I want it to be night. I feel encumbered by time, objects and space. I wish there was no visual burden for me to bear. I wish this closet didn't have these handles that shine so brightly in the day. I wish I could tuck this bed into the wall. I want to throw all the books out of his room. I want it to be so dark the only way to see is artificial light. I want there to be nothing, nothing but us, not even sound. Every sense I possess is overstimulated, but I don't feel dread. I don't.

"What do you feel then, if not dread?" He asked.

"Resignation, but it's not sad," I told him, "There is a moment when you realise the things that are going to happen to you, will happen, no matter what you do, you're powerless, I see that now."

"That does sound sad though," he said, clearly aroused by my despair, which is my favourite thing about his arousal, it digs deep.

"It's not," I told him, "Because after you really accept that you are powerless, you don't have to care about what is going to happen anymore."

"So you don't care anymore?" He asked, reaching over to touch my face.

"No, destroy me, I deserve it and even if I don't it is not for me to decide," I responded, "Really, there's only one actual problem I have."

"What is that?" He asked, truly hoping he could solve it.

"The sun," I told him.

The bright, natural realism of the sun has got to go. The artificiality of a dim, yellow dust-covered lightbulb that should have been changed years ago is the only lighting in which my story makes sense.

...

I feel a sense of quiet devotion. I cleaned our room, changed the sheets, removed all the clutter from every corner of the room and prepared the space for him to destroy me later. He is planning something elaborate and extensive and I like being made to clean the space where I will be massacred. It's like having the criminal prepare their own noose for slaughter. It's an unnecessary evil, the kind that abounds in times of war when morality is but a bloodied scrap of cloth at the bottom of the gutter.

As I prepared the room, he sat on the bed cutting a section of white cloth from an old apron. He made me write on it.

"I deserve to be punished."

...

"Are you upset because I don't seem to be suffering?" I asked him, as he dropped a mallet on my thighs, repeatedly, from two-feet above.

I had been completely quiet all evening. I think a part of it was caused by the fact that there was this cloth covering my mouth. It didn't keep me from talking, it wasn't inside my mouth or pulled over my mouth in any way that truly impeded speech but sometimes the suggestion of silencing is enough to silence. Sometimes just because you hold a finger up to your lips, the silence feels enforced. When I finally spoke, I was surprised that I could speak.

"I *am* upset that you don't seem to be suffering," he said, dropping the mallet from a greater height.

It hurt very much. However, as I looked back, to all those days of screaming, fighting and crying, I was confused by my own behaviour. I realise that I have just adjusted to the intensity of his unrelenting attacks and the state of physical intensity, but despite that knowledge, I feel like a fool for how I was acting earlier. Screaming, sniveling, crying. How can you even be sorry if you fight your sentence? If you keep hoping to stop it, if you scream and fight your suffering, are you really as repentant as you should be? I feel that now, because the dread has been deracinated from my heart and in its wake it has left a heartbroken resolve to make a play for some kind of dignity in this suffering.

I sat through it quietly as he stitched the piece of white cloth that read, "*I deserve to be punished*" over my mouth. He put five stitches on either side to hold it in place. Each time he put the suture needle through my skin, then through the cloth and then back through my skin again, I expected myself to squeeze the arms of the chair, grit my teeth or whimper out loud, but the needle felt like it was passing through water. I couldn't get enough of it. I love the pain of a needle going through my skin and because of the surgical skills he acquired at his job, I enjoy watching how he works with needles and sutures. The way he does knots and patterns is so wonderfully alien to me, I can marvel at it like it's magic. I would never let anyone else do it to me, but it would be foolish not to reap the benefits of a maxillofacial surgeon as the partner of a facial-abuse fetishist.

You realise life doesn't, or shouldn't, often come around so fucking poetically perfect, right? That's what is most terrifying about being with him. I am often left taking a step back, looking at us, and wondering — How is this possible? How is it actually possible that we found each other? I spent my life seeking the romance of a fist to my face, taking anyone who would be willing to brutalise me and then I met a man who could break my jaw, and then fix it. He could x-ray my face on an annual basis and study the long-term effects of slapping on the facial bone-structure and it would genuinely benefit his academic pursuits. You couldn't find a better subject to do that with than me. I have the freedom to trust him so completely with my face because he's the actual expert on facial trauma. Tell me how I should justify not believing in magic? I cannot.

After he finished stitching my plight to my face, he dragged me from the chair to the bed and brought the mallet. He began to drop it on my thighs. Over and over. The pain was emanating from deep inside, it's very different from the pain of a cane, it bruises much deeper, it gets to the skin much slower, but it debilitates much quicker. Yesterday, maybe I would have screamed and begged, but today, I couldn't remember why I would do anything but silently endure every single thing he gave to me. If for no reason other than the fact that I must need to be punished for all the screaming and the noise to which I have subject him for days. I wanted him to know though, I wanted him to know that I was holding my silence for him. That is why I asked him about his feelings about my lack of apparent suffering, I was hoping he would tell me that he knew I was suffering, but I was just determined to behave. Instead he said that he was upset I wasn't suffering and it made my brain itch. How can you stitch someone's face and then drop hammers on them and actually believe they aren't suffering? How can you? How?

"Do you know why I appear not to be suffering?" I asked him.

"I probably am not hurting you enough," he said, "Your skin and your tissues aren't reacting to this instantly, I cannot see your suffering, so it doesn't feel like suffering."

I broke into tears in one second. The moment he said it I started to cry like a child with big, fat tears that rolled down the sides of my face and into my pigtails like a river in the monsoon. How could he really think he wasn't hurting me enough? Is my suffering really only visible to him through my skin and my tissues? Can he not see it in my adherence to the silence he imposes upon me? Can he not hear it in the quickening of my breath? Can he not sense it in my performative resolve? Does he not see me at all? Am I nothing to him but flesh? Deep inside, in the place still capable of reason and deconstruction, I knew he was only saying that to hurt me. I knew he wanted to disregard all that I was doing to please him just to punish my soul for all its hopeless little errors over the past few days, but in the shallowness of my heart, I couldn't see that. All I could think about was that he didn't see me, he didn't see any measure of a person in me at all. Nothing but skin and tissues. Disappointing skin and tissues.

I cried so much I think I scared him. He leaned over to me and watched me as I began to mutter incoherently. I oscillated between apologies for being perpetually disappointing and questions about what I had to do to finally earn his approval. There was such rawness to my heart, such sorrowful vulnerability, I think I stopped making sense. Yet even as he spoke to me about my little outbreak, and I demanded with unearned valour that he see me, he kept beating me. The last time he stopped, I remember him coming over to sit beside me, I remember talking for a very long time. I remember crying so much, my eyes still hurt. I remember begging him not to apologise for hurting my feelings. That's why they exist. My feelings exist for him to hurt. I just wish he had understood them quicker.

Yet, I knew, didn't I? I knew we would get here, to this place where playing with my broken body would feel so quaint and juvenile, I cannot even remember why it hurt so much when he beat my back or my breasts or my thighs.

It has nothing on this.

He broke my fucking heart and I can't even scream. I won't. I must grieve hope in silence. The sun is gone now, isn't it? It's what I wanted.

...

Day 8

I woke up with a headache. I didn't sleep very much at all. These somatic disturbances are part of the design, the bodily responses I cannot control, the erosion of strength, the lack of sleep and they make me feel hollow. After he went to bed, I spent hours writing and then thinking about everything that had happened between us. I could not believe how much I had cried earlier.

I cry with relish, most often when I am being penetrated, but at times also when I am being beaten or otherwise tortured, I cry most vigorously when he succeeds at truly breaking my heart, and all those kinds of tears feel different inside me. The tears I cry when he is fucking me and hurting the insides of my cunt, are the easiest. They just emerge. Even when I am at my most aroused and genuinely desirous of being fucked, those tears cannot be avoided. Of course, he has encouraged those tears, fetishized them, rubbed his cock against them and made me drink them, so many times, over the years. Nothing will ever compare to the pleasure of being groomed, I came into this relationship with a half-broken cunt that liked to be tortured and he laid waste to it. He laid waste to me. While another may have dismantled my extant systems, he conquered them. He took them over, greedily usurping my trauma from the others who had left their stamp and turning it into his plaything. I always hated being fucked, he made me dread it. He took away even the pretence of my pleasure, he made no attempt to fix it or enhance it, he turned it into a ritualistic act of dispassion to be fucked by him. We are never more distant than when he is inside me.

Last night, I found myself longing to reach over to him and begging him to make love to me; I wanted to feel him hold me while he was inside me, I wanted to be able to look into his eyes and cry, I wanted him to kiss me or at least, bite my neck. Just put his mouth on me like he remembers that in some version of this story, we are lovers. I worried that if I woke him up and told him that, he would beat me and then demonstratively fuck me in a manner that was the opposite of what I desired. I don't think I would have survived that, although, I would not have had a choice. So, I just lay beside him and longed. I thought about my tears. The tears of pain are different from the tears of being fucked. They are a relief, a Hail Mary when you've run out of all solutions, an admittance of the helplessness to the pain that helps you get through it.

But the tears of emotional pain are harrowing.

Heartbreak, hopelessness, resignation, all of these things and more, the implements of emotional masochism, elicit a reaction from the human repository of sorrow. To be hurt like that on purpose, and to be made to continue to hurt even after you have broken, is the kind of cruelty that keeps you up at night. It makes you feel sorry for yourself. When I open myself up to being so vulnerable, vulnerable enough to admit that I am overpowered by emotion and unable to rein myself, and he steps on my heart in that state, it feels like having my skin peeled off before being thrown into a septic tank. Last night he threw me into the tank, and then he fell asleep, as I lay there still hurting. Still crying. Still longing.

For more?

What is wrong with me?

...

When he came in from walking the dog this morning, I was sitting at the breakfast table with the kid ordering birthday presents for him. It's in 20-days. Every year, I try to keep what I am getting him a secret, but every year, some comedy of errors ends up revealing what I am getting for him. Last year it was the kid who told him, I was getting him a smart television (because apparently people still want giant screens in their lives), and I told the kid about it, I also told him that if he told his father, I wouldn't let him watch the television. His father asked him, persistently, and he held his own for a few hours.

"Bro I can't tell you," the kid said finally, exasperated, "If I tell you, A won't let me watch the TV."

It took him a long moment to realise what he had done. God, why must I live with *boys*. This year I am getting him a bar because he wants the ritual and decor that comes with recreational inebriation. Seriously, I don't get the fixation of alcohol-enthusiasts on the equipment, on extensive cabinets and wine racks, but I know he feels it, I am happy to feed it. I kept it hidden for weeks and he has been trying to guess for just as long. I had been refusing to answer all questions, but I inadvertently admitted that I was waiting until the beginning of the month to order it, he figured I was waiting to be paid and somehow that led him to concluding I was getting him a bar. I think he went through my phone or saw over my shoulder at some point and has been sitting on the information.

I started to eagerly tell him about my plans for him bar. I got a nice huge cabinet with a mixing shelf and a wine rack for storage, a wall-mounted shelf for glasses and a really cool bar trolley. I got some posters and lights, I'm thinking I'll put one of my invisible bookshelves in the space and fill it with Bukowski and Hemingway. They're the correct choice of writers for a bar. Maybe I should get some stools as well. I like stools. They're my favorite. He listened to my enthusiastic plans and then as he walked past me to the bedroom, he bent over and kissed me on the head.

"Today, I'm going to beat you with barbed wire, cunt," he whispered into my ear before he left.

I forgot all about the bar.

I forgot all about the world.

That's what I wanted, right?

...

He's fucking my cunt with objects again. I knew, obviously I knew, that yesterday's excusal of my cunt didn't have to do with compassion, but with the need to allow enough recovery that I could be consistently hurt again. I would hate how thoughtfully he approaches maximizing pain if I wasn't so impressed by it. He put me over the bed while I was taking a break from working and fucked me with the dildo again. I don't know why I keep expecting that it will get easier to bear. I want to yell at myself for refusing to learn. Why cant I learn?

I didn't thrash around though, I didn't scream very much, I didn't cry and I didn't beg him to stop. I think the begging has to stop, I think that on his behalf, I think I am about to get beaten for begging too much very soon if I don't put it away. I just dug my own nails into my palms as he fucked me. I used to do that a lot, I wonder when I stopped, I wonder why I stopped.

"It's almost pointless to punish your cunt for still daring to be wet," he said, thrusting inside me.

His manner was almost, bored. It wasn't taking him very much effort to hurt me so much. I'm just made of pain now. I cannot remember what it felt like not to hurt. My thighs hurt, my back hurts, my cunt hurts, my face hurts, my head hurts. Tomorrow some of those parts will recover and some other parts will join the list, my cunt will be a permanent resident of the list but it will all hurt, it constantly hurts.

"It's you, you're the problem," he said, pulling the dildo out in its entirety and shoving it back it's full length each time,

"Punishing your cunt won't fix you, it probably would learn, but you won't let it."

Sometimes, he creates two characters in me, my entire self and his cunt, he pits us against each other and makes my situation dependent on acquiescing to the demands of his cunt. It has favour with him, I do not. That doesn't mean he treats it better, it means he expects it to understand why it must be treated poorly to the end of my repentance. He makes it want that as much as he does. It knows how to behave, I do not. It does his bidding to keep me in line, I resist it. Sometimes, they take on such lucid forms that they have conversations with each other, shamefully lurid conversations, that I will never, ever repeat. I only repeat them for him, when he draws them out by teasing me to a state where I can feel nothing in my body but my cunt in arousal, it's very different from this state, but it's just as harrowing. Maybe later, I will tell you about it.

When he exonerated my cunt while holding me responsible for all the punishment I deserve, I moaned out loud in arousal, the shooting pain of pleasure that began in the tip of my clit travelled inside me like a bullet. It hurts to be turned on.

"Does it hurt to get horny, cunt?" He asked me as I wrapped my arms around my abdomen, hoping to ease a cramp I couldn't reach.

"Yes master," I croaked, "I am sorry, I am useless and disappointing."

"You are," he said, fucking me harder with the dildo, "But don't worry, by the end of this, it will hurt so much to be turned on, you'll rip your hair out before you try it."

That cannot really happen.

It can't.

No.

...

Yesterday, while he beat me with the hammer I asked him how he experienced enjoyment while hurting me if he insists on having me be silent and non-responsive. A part of the answer, the part about my compliance to the standard being the heart of his enjoyment, I expected. The rest of it was a surprise.

"Your screams and tears is not where I see your pain, for the most part," he explained, "You're inconsistent anyway, sometimes you are quiet even though I am cleaving your flesh, sometimes you scream even though all I did was put a single finger in you."

I would have argued that it was a false equivalency that he was following, but he would have just beat me harder for objecting to being gaslit.

"So where do you see my pain?" I asked.

"In your flesh," he said, pounding the mallet against my thighs, "In the response of your skin and your tissues. In the sound of the cane or the hammer, pounding against your skin. That's why it's so annoying when you insist on being noisy, I cannot hear the actual sounds I want to hear."

"So when you beat me, you don't want to hear me, you want to hear...the cane?" I asked him.

"Yes, obviously," he said, "What good is hearing you?"

I don't know which of his words are true anymore and which ones are being said explicitly to hurt me, even the ones that feel like lies have the quality of truths, and the ones that seem true, make me wish they were lies. I wished desperately that he cared more about my reactions than the sound and responses of my flesh, but he has spent years training me into silence. It didn't feel as terrible when I believed it was because my obedience was getting him hard, now it feels like being erased and muted so he can watch and hear something else. I feel like the girl he is fucking so he has a hole to come in while watching the pornography he really enjoys that is playing in the back. How am I being cuckolded by myself?

When he bent me over the bed to beat me this evening, I kept thinking about his answers from yesterday. He was beating me with the baseball bat wrapped in barbed wire, as far as reactions of skin and sound go, it's a sensory orgy to use this horrifying implement. I was quiet, but I didn't want to be, usually I want nothing more than to be pliant, pathetic creature that gives him exactly what he demands, but I couldn't stop thinking about what he had told me yesterday. I kept wishing I could scream, I kept wondering how it would feel to be the girl who is allowed to scream, whose screams and reactions are relished instead of punished.

But I didn't dare scream.

Not only because I am not sure what the penalty is for being disagreeable when you're already being beaten with a bat wrapped in barbed wire, and I don't want to find out, but also because I still do really want to be the mythical exemplary slave he touts before me like a prodigal child I must live up to. I will always fail, but he makes it seem possible, so I will always try as well. Besides, it is easiest for me not to scream when I can feel the blood pouring out of my skin. I get so lost in it, I forget I am attached to the same body. It occured to me, while he was beating me, that we should name the bat. I wanted to call it Morticia. If I am Wednesday, the bat feels like it should be Morticia, wielded by the hands of Gomez. It was an idle thought, it got lost in the thousands of other idle thoughts I had.

After he finished, he said we should name the bat. He suggested we call it Batricia. Like Morticia, but in bat form. Could he hear my thoughts in my blood?

Tell me how I should believe there is no magic.

...

The second beating was a surprise. We were in bed, beside each other, and we were having a long, emotional conversation. I was crying, he was as vulnerable as I was and we were both so woefully exposed to each other that an eavesdropper would have to cover their eyes just to keep themselves from exploding from the intrusion. I was crying so much. I have been crying so fucking much, surely I'll run out of tears soon? He was being kind to me, he was consoling me for all the pain he has caused me without reassuring me about any of it. He wouldn't do that. He will see it through. He will ensure I get to the end of this, screaming or crying or dragged through the streets or dead, he won't pretend it will get easier.

But he was being kind.

I was feeling trapped and alone in an isolated state of mind. I was feeling like I was reeling by myself and my tormenter, the only other creature I could recognise had left the building. He hadn't actually abandoned me, but it is a.. sentiment. It's easier, in a way for the enforcer, to step back for a moment and sink into relief. Their bodies and minds aren't going through it the same way, it's actually possible for them to pretend the world still exists, it's possible for them to live in it.

"I love you," he was telling me, wiping my tears from my ears, "I love you very much, I will not let you feel abandoned in this space, okay?"

"Please get on top of me?" I begged him.

He did. At first, he lay on top of me, crushing my chest with his weight as he kissed my chin. I winced and cried out. As soon as I made those sounds, he sat up on my thighs. I yelped. The damage from the hammer is so, so deep. The flesh on my thighs is hard and swollen, I can see the bruises travel towards it from so deep inside, it looks like all of my skin has taken on a tinge of purple. He sat down so hard on my thighs, it made me scream.

"Are you hurting me on purpose?" I asked, as he squeezed his knees shut against my hips.

"Always," he said, putting more weight on my thighs.

I wriggled and cried.

"Are you really going to be disappointing even as a seat?" He said, squeezing his knees shut to hold me in place, "Do you never tire of being completely fucking useless?"

I was about to bawl but he punched me first. He punched me so hard, I was stunned into silence. I couldn't believe he was actually beating me again, I really thought we were done for the day. He started slapping me and in the second slap I bit the inside of my lip and blood squirted into my mouth. I brought my hand to my face to protect it, it was instinctive, but I also put it back down before he could say anything.

"If you try to protect your face again, I will break your fucking wrist, you understand me?" He said, holding my wrist and twisting it just a little.

"Yes master," I responded in a blind panic, "I am sorry, I won't try to protect myself."

"You won't? You cannot!" He exclaimed, slapping me with alarming pace, "I will beat you as much as you fucking deserve, or can you not even do penance right?"

I couldn't respond to him because my mouth was too busy being slapped by his knuckles. His ring hit my canine. I hate the sound of teeth and metal.

"You are so, so disappointing," he said digging the knife already lodged into my throat, "Truly, terrible slave."

There was a dialogue on Veep, where the character of Amy says: *I feel like I am on life support and they keep pulling the plug to charge their phones.* That's how he was making me feel.

Finally, he got off me and lay back down beside me.

"Are you in a lot of pain?" He asked.

I nodded my head.

"Remember that, as the least amount of pain you will have been in tomorrow," he said, the sentence made too little sense, and too much.

If I stay awake all night, can I stop tomorrow from coming?

...

Day 9

There is festivity in the air this morning. Holi is very big where we live. It's so big that it's not a day, it's a season and people come from all over the country to experience the Holi of this city. Everyone is off work, everyone is excited and drugged, there are colours in the air and sweets in the offing, and I feel like my gaze is turning the whole world black.

As it should be, really. If you see a red door, you know what to do.

I woke up wanting to be on my knees. As soon as my eyes opened, I wanted to slide off the bed and kneel on the floor. I felt some uneasiness in my chest, like a secret you know will keep haunting you until you admit to it, and I couldn't wait for him to wake up so I could admit it to him. I know where all of my guilt resides now — in emotion and imperfection — I've been reviewing the daily lists I have made and there are such clear patterns to my guilt. I believe I have no right to a reaction. I have no right to inconvenience the world with my emotions. I must not be upset when something upsets me. I must never get angry. In a room full of people, I must cater to the emotions of all, while never revealing that I have any. Even if I am going through something, I believe that the emotions of the stakeholders in my life in response to what is happening to me are more permitted and valid than mine. It's how I was raised. If you were ill, it didn't matter what you were feeling, you had to get better because you were inconveniencing your parents into worrying about you.

A thousand little things and a dozen big ones reinforced this message to me so strongly, I now spend my life apologising for my emotions. I am *shocked* when things actually impact me. I tell my husband that all the time, whenever I actually have an emotional reaction that is strong enough for me to take note of or to actively emote, I tell him that I cannot believe that things actually impact me. I really cannot believe it because I always do the math first, I calculate the emotion that is reasonable to feel and then I solve the emotion by introducing an established solution or an inevitability that I have to accept, and then it's resolved. When things linger past this process, I feel guilty for wasting my time and the potential attention of other people in my life on useless things. I do not believe my emotions are allowed, I think they are wasteful, and I carry around a world of guilt for feeling them anyway.

And then there is the imperfection.

I have decided that I cannot do anything wrong and everything that doesn't pass the test is an active reason to diminish myself and my value. If I didn't work for eight hours today, I would be useless. If I felt tired even at the end of the day, I would be useless. I have to sleep because it is a non-optional bodily convention, not because I am tired. If I rest because of tiredness, I have failed. None of it is allowed. All failure is completely unacceptable and everything less than an unflinching standard of perfection is failure. I am scrutinizing my behaviour at a level where I will deem myself a failure for thoughts of failure. If I even considered not going to the gym today, but then actually went, I would consider that a failure. If I considered taking a day off for absolutely no reason, I would consider myself useless. These exacting standards, which I would be happy to blame on my mother but aren't really entirely her fault, are keeping me from living more intuitively to my own detriment. I will never be perfect by my yardstick and perhaps it is time to question who the yardstick even serves. What is the goal of this yardstick? What would happen if I were to actually attain perfection? Clearly, it would be the most anti-climactic part of the story, which is why I keep shifting the goal-post. I know there is nothing there. I keep doing it because I want to feel the guilt.

I needed him to wake him so I could beg him to punish me for having emotions and being imperfect.

I know that sounds like I have learnt the wrong lesson but let's not be bogged down by simplistic reasoning and generic, monolithic solutions. In the past eight days, the locus of my guilt has been actively sexual. He has been punishing me unrelentingly for and with every emotion he does not allow me to have, every reaction that demands I be seen in my humanity and every lapse of perfection no matter how minuscule. As a result I've been able to continue experiencing enough guilt to not panic while I observe the inner-workings of my treatment of myself. At that point, it would be detrimental for me to tell myself to just stop feeling guilty, it would be like telling a person with nine fingers to just grow another one, but I can manipulate the guilt into a sphere where it serves me, and in the vacated sphere of my emotional mechanisms, I can finally do some actual work. And it, somehow, is working.

I didn't guide him, nor did I know all of this so clearly when we started, but somehow our interactions naturally led to this place. This is my favourite thing about both sexual/romantic relationships and writing, you never know where the story will go when you start writing it. There's a Nigerian writer named Akwaeke Emezi. In an interview, she was talking about writing a romance novel right after she finished working on a work of speculative fiction. She said she started writing it because she thought it would be relaxing and fun, but she came to realise through the process how the formulaic nature of romance writing was hurting the genre because even though her approach to the characters she was writing started off as callous, at some point the characters demanded they be harked in their entirety.

"Bitch, I have depths," she quoted her character as having said to her.

That's the nature of writing, sex and love that makes me love life. You don't know, ever, where any of it will go but the process of discovery is filled with wonderment. I don't know how my husband and I came to be here, and in these things, in writing, sex and love, I do not feel the same pressure to take charge and make it all happen. I don't feel worried about perfection and curation. I don't even think about how it will all come together. The magic is not in what happens, it's in how it happens. It's in the interactions. In the moments in between action, whether as I write or fuck, when I sit quietly with my eyes closed because I wouldn't be able to absorb all of it if I didn't. I wouldn't be able to feel its immensity in motion, nor in active thought, it has to pass through me. That is the most pleasurable moment of life. It's the one that matters to me the most. Maybe it is, meaning. Maybe that is why, despite all of my neurotic tendencies, these spaces of my life remain uninfringed. I am safe from my own judgement in these spaces because I recognise their value to a point where even if I doubt it, I won't question it, because I am not big enough, nor vast enough, to know everything that needs to be known to make that decision. I deify love and writing to the point where I really need no other god. In them, I am free.

And by bringing my guilt into these rooms to observe and understand, I have allowed myself to experience some of this freedom in other spheres of my existence. In the past nine days, I have slept in and felt perfectly okay about it. I have enforced boundaries with people for the sole purpose of my well-being. I have distorted my work schedules and timings in ways I would never dream of having done a month ago, and you know? Everything got done anyway and I didn't have to be stressed. I have challenged my perpetual need to seek validation in the form of assent for my existence from people who refuse to see the world for all its problems. I have skipped the gym with no self-loathing inner monologue. I have allowed myself to waver from unrelenting discipline because its purpose is becoming unclear and its enforcement has gotten so harsh, I can see now why it exists only because I need enough reasons to keep yelling at myself. I will not work through all of the guilt in fourteen days, but I am building mechanisms I never thought I would be courageous enough to attempt.

So I had to wake him up.

To punish me.

...

The Sterillium just lives at my desk now. For a while I kept putting it back in the closet in my quest to get rid of every little bit of clutter, but he needs to disinfect me (and the rest of his toys) so often these days I have to take it back out five times a day. It just lives here now.

I think he will kill me today. I think today is the day I die.

He has been caning my thighs every hour. It only takes five minutes because he only does it ten times each time, but it feels like he is setting me on fire every sixty minutes to test various accelerants. It's happened four times already since this morning and I don't think it stops until I go to bed. Unless he intends to have me wake up every hour and cane myself ten times. Which I would do.

It should hurt more.

I keep thinking that, and I now realise it's because I have been sitting up, able to see my thighs, while he administers these canings. I think seeing the impact coming makes it easier to bear, somehow, he says it's because your eyes are telling your brain to brace for impact and it's able to calculate how strong the impact will be and make the necessary adjustments to get through it in time. I think it's kindness, but it's probably accidental. He wasn't very kind when I looked at him in surprise two canings ago when he put the cane down and began to punch my arms afterwards. It was a momentary lapse in judgment, it was naive of me to assume that just because he is caning me every hour, he wouldn't hurt me any other way and my face betrayed my surprise before I had the chance to rein in that emotion. He took issue with it.

"You will take whatever the fuck I give you," he said, holding my face in his hand, "The only response you will have is to thank me and nothing else, do you fucking understand? The nice guy from last week isn't here anymore."

The nice guy? The *nice* guy? I think he is audacious in his approach. In the moment, it's attractive and after the fact, it's amusing. As a concept, his estimation of himself is appalling. Still, he is right, he is much more cruel than he was last week. I knew this would happen, my body is just a means to get to what he really wants to break, my heart, and I am worn down now. I have no defences. I am all emotion, obedience and despair. These are his favourite toys. He has been testing it, telling me to do things, not big things, not even tasks really, just notions. He's been telling me to stand up, go out of the room, put on shoes or bend over, and relishing the fact that I just do it without even taking a beat to question or wonder why. I can feel his thrill as I obey him without any resistance at all. Not even resistance of thought or reflex inside my own head.

I can also feel my thrill.

I am drawn to a state of unquestioning obedience and I don't really enjoy having that state extracted by ethical or compassionate means. I want to be eroded, coerced and rendered helpless. I want him to conjure the circumstances that defeat me like a majestic act of theatre into which I am thrust without script or preparation. I want him to direct me without consulting me. The resultant state of my heart, of my behaviour, is like a drug my body forgets and is surprised by each time it is administered again. I feel unencumbered by the world, how does it matter to me? All that matters is that I stand when he tells me to stand. How copacetic it is to be able to embody this state, where I can forget about meaning and structure, and exist only to stand if told.

...

After the last caning, he fucked me with the dildo and then with his fingers. I think I asked for it. After he put the cane down, I leaned backwards, as if to suggest that I should lay down on my back. He pushed me into the bed, fucked me with his fingers and then pushed the dildo inside me. I think he intended to just leave it there because he enjoys knowing that I am filled up in a hole where I hate it, for no reason except that he wants me to keep passively hurting. After he pushed it in, he seemed to retreat.

I rolled over onto my stomach and lifted my hips up to him myself. It was an act of shame that I performed because I wanted to feel the arousal elicited by the shame. It felt a little sick to brandish myself like this, to go to him so I can make a pornographic display of my confession to arousal, but

I wanted to do it so much. I wanted to tell him that I won't stop being a dirty, filthy whore who is turned on by her own state of disgrace so much that even the complete destruction of her holes won't stop her from wanting more.

And he did give it to me.

I didn't fight it at all that time. I felt the panic, the blind urgency to make him evacuate my cunt, the instant sense of shame and amends, I felt all of it, but none of it turned into reaction. I just lay there and took it, my cunt made me do it. It made me ask him for more. It made me prostrate my need to feel punished and make a pathetic display of it. I stayed in that position for a long time after he stopped, with my hips pushed up in the air, and my cunt leaking onto my thighs. He walked around humiliating me. Telling me how disappointing and disgusting I was to make a display like this.

The humiliation was always coming, I know that, but he is the worst of himself when that's his goal. I want the sun now. Can I keep it from being night?

...

Each time he pulled the soaking wet section of cloth off my face or I pulled it off myself because of the panic, the first thing I would see, was the bulge in his shorts. The first time I thought I was imagining it, the second time I tried to convince myself that it was the light and the angle that made it seem like an erection but soon enough, it became impossible to deny. Waterboarding me was making him hard.

I don't know how I feel about that.

The first spray of the water felt like the water always does. Whether it is the rain or the ocean, the first spray always feels like coming home. I'm surprised I don't have gills, but it became very clear, very quickly, that I do not have gills. In one second, it went from the refreshment of being alive to the abject horror of drowning. Years ago, when I used to be on board with my father, we would walk on the deck in the evenings and he would teach me all manners of superstitions and adages of sailors. One of his favourite things to tell me was that the ocean is like a disloyal woman, you will love her with a madness that makes you feel alive, but she will eat you alive if you trust her even a little bit. No one in my family ever took that class where they teach you what is appropriate to tell your kids and what is not.

"Love the water, Sickness," he used to say, using the strange little hypocorism he still uses for me today, "But the moment you trust it, it will kill you."

My relationship with the water is so heavily informed by his, from the enthusiasm to the romanticism, my terrified, deferential love of the water is my inheritance from my father. And perhaps it is that inheritance that led me to the man I love, as well. He is the ocean. He loves me and he holds enough destruction to kill me in an instant. I love him but it is idiocy to let my guard down around him. He holds all of my peace and all of the power to take it away. He makes me feel alive and he takes away my breath.

God, how he took away my breath.

I do not like to be waterboarded. I've drowned enough before to know how it feels, it's not comparable to much else in the world. In comparison — all the fists, the canes, the baseball bats — they're child's play. There is the possibility for him to tell me to be quiet and take it when he beats me, because he can still access the person I am in that state of suffering. There is no person when you are drowning, there is only the human will to fight for its life. You cannot hide from this panic, you cannot meditate the terror away, you cannot grasp at your skin to distract your brain. If you are drowning, you can focus only on the fact that you are drowning. I was not a person, I was not his slave, I was not even myself, I was just drowning.

In seconds, it took mere seconds, for the panic to turn into an attempt to get away. I didn't fight him, but I tried to fight the water. Which, I know, is futile. I have the words tattooed on my ankle — *Don't fight the ocean* — yet I tried. I tried so hard I thrashed around in his grasp, I tried to pull the cloth off my face, again and again. He kicked me and put it back every single time. I tried to communicate that this dread, this insidious fear, it wasn't the erotic allure of dangerous, it was the human will fighting not to die, but he didn't seem to care.

His cock was hard.

I really don't know how I feel about that. I know it turns him on to hurt me. I know it turns him on to beat me, torture me, humiliate me, torment me and reduce my heart to rubble, all of that just feels like the love of a sadist. This didn't feel like love. It didn't feel like romance. It didn't feel like sadism. It felt like he was getting off to threatening me with death, in some ways it felt like the furthest reaches of his cruelty, and that erection felt like it was mocking me. It felt like it was showing me that he wasn't going to give me any mercy, why would he? Why would he even offer me the respite of lying bent over the floor for him to fuck when he could get all his sexual pleasure from tormenting me with the sensation of death?

He dragged me across the bathroom floor, to the other end and propped me against the wall. The soaking wet cloth rested on my head. He punched me and kicked me while I cried and begged. It didn't hurt very much, but really, I couldn't take anymore, I couldn't take anymore of anything at all. Even the disgruntled expression on his face, the one that has been telling me everyday that I am disappointing, felt like a hot iron skewer through the heart. As he reached over to pull the cloth back over my head, I began to beg so earnestly, I almost felt sorry for myself. I thought for sure that he would heed my calls for mercy, I could feel in my own face that I had never begged like that before in my entire life.

"You want me to stop, is it?" He asked, holding my face by the chin, "I will stop when I fucking please and you will shut the fuck up and take it. Pull the cloth back over your face."

I did it. It didn't feel like I had much choice. I had to do what the water told me to do. I fought even harder, I kept coming back and pulling it off my face, and he kept beating me and forcing me to put it back in place. At one point it felt like my tears were adding to the flood and I was drowning in them as well. Each time he pulled the cloth off, I begged, each time I begged, my stupid little heart really believed that he would stop. Despite all evidence, I kept on believing. He kept up showing me that I am a fool.

I've made a huge mistake.

I've trusted the water. Now it's going to kill me.

...

Day 10

I woke up this morning because someone was testing the speakers for their Holi party. Punjabi music was blaring out of speakers that could stand to be repaired or thrown away altogether. The song was so familiar, the kind of cultural institution that is indisputable and unbearable; it was the kind of song that no one ever plays for themselves, but everyone knows all the words to, and everyone will beg for it to be played at parties. Dance is so important to social rituals in our country. Sometimes I wonder what the Indian identity means to me, and while I keep coming up with the constitution as the only acceptable answer for myself, I think I discount certain cultural aspects of identity. Like spices and dancing. What is India, really? The individual spice palettes of every state seem to form the conglomerate that constitutes its fingerprint. The myriad excuses to dance in different ways, for different reasons, at different times of day; there is a melody to the way we exist, there is rhythm, and every political distortion of divide is an arrhythmia, but that break in the pattern isn't what sullies Indian identity, it's part of it. We're a vibrant, lovely tapestry with heart disease. The horrible is much who we are as the wonderful.

As I resolved and failed repeatedly to go back to sleep, he stirred beside me. He turned around and put his arm around me. I tried to adjust my arm but he grabbed my wrist and held it to the bed. I could feel his erection against my thigh. In a few moments he went back to gently snoring, but my wrist remained fastened by his grip, like I was chained in wait, of the inevitable impalement. The song changed to another one of those Punjabi songs. It reminded me of a bar I used to frequent fourteen-years ago. It was halfway between school and my home, but that's not why I went there. I wasn't even that much of a drinker, but there was something forbidden about working-class watering holes. Forbidden to women, that is, and I didn't quite know how to articulate this then, but I was seeking to impose my right to loitering space. When you're a young woman growing up in a conservative culture, no matter how progressive your household may be, you have to contend with the mores of society and so much of them were to do with what girls could and could not do.

We couldn't wear this or that. We had to be home at a certain hour. We had to be polite to men because you couldn't hurt a male ego. We had to dumb ourselves down because we would scare the men otherwise. We couldn't just express sexual interest in people lest we have our reputations ruined, it was mandatory to perform the dance of reluctance and emotion for every dick we wanted in us. We couldn't go to bars like that one. Those bars were for the men and to go alone, all bars were for men. I wanted that space. I knew that the only long-term plan to emancipate myself was to wait till I was a legal adult, a high-school graduate and able to make all decisions for myself, but in the meanwhile, for the few intervening years, I needed to be able to make a play for some kind of free.

That bar was freedom to me.

I used to go there so often, they let me do whatever I wanted and I know a certain sensibility is bound to wonder why they weren't perturbed by the underage girl in the bar and it is simple. First of all that rule was barely enforced back then and second the pornographic view society is allowed to have of young women in general made them want me their. I was an aberration. A spectacle. A wayward girl. They wanted to watch me like a dirty train wreck.

I was dirty.

I am a confident person but in that phase in my life I possessed a kind of toxic sexual confidence that was unshakeable. Look, I am not proud of it, but the awareness that no matter what happened the fact that I would always be the underage one in that equation, emboldened me to fearlessness. The fact that I had already, in my life, let a man get away with raping me and convincing me that I had somehow been wrong to allow it, had me on a vengeful rampage. I would find men at the bar and take them to the mostly abandoned back stairway. I barely said a few words to them before I asked them if they wanted to fuck, I enjoyed how startled men are by that. They think you are crazy, but it scares them too. If they said yes, I would lead them to the staircase and push them against the wall. They'd try to kiss me but I would drop to my knees and unzip their pants. I'd hold their wrists against the wall while I sucked their cocks. I'd ask them to pull my hair, choke me, push me against the wall and fuck me. All of it, at my instruction. All of my pleasure, delivered to the letter, as I wrote it.

And then later when I saw them again at the bar, I would mix them up. Forgetting which cock was inside me on which day of which week, I had no qualms about showing my confusion.

Some of them told stories about me, turning my presence in that bar into a show they would summon other men to witness, but it wasn't the blatant sexuality I carried that scared them, I know, it was the fact that I wasn't scared of them. The fact that I came into that bar and acted like I had the right to belong. That I didn't need them for anything except my pleasure. I was at my most fearless when I grabbed men by the wrist and pushed them into the wall.

I am at my most fearful when he grabs my wrist.

There are messaging systems in place between us, ones that evolved slowly over years of flirtatious exchanges and heart-wrenching exposure, I know what he means when he touches me a certain way. When he strokes my chin with his thumb, he is about to slap me. When he takes his watch off hours before bed, he is about to beat me. When he strokes the lower part of my back he wants me to bend over. When he grabs my wrist, he is going to fuck me. I knew it was coming. In time he began to grab my wrist harder and pulled himself over me. As he pushed both my wrists into the bed and opened his eyes to my terror, I couldn't help but think back to all the years of demanding a fucking from the men before me. Of screaming in throes of need that they weren't hurting me nearly at all. *Fuck me harder, fuck me harder.*

And now.

"Please don't fuck me," I begged him.

It's not just dreadful anymore, its elegiac, like every fucking is a swan song. He laughed at me and twisted my wrists, sitting down harder on my sore thighs and pressing into them hard enough for me to remember this game isn't over. God, it isn't over at all.

"Shut the fuck up, ungrateful ingrate," he said, gritting his teeth, "I was so nice to you all night."

That is a half-truth. At midnight, after he was done beating me, waterboarding me and torturing my cunt, I begged him to be nice to me for the rest of the night. I corrected and explained that he didn't even have to take care of me, I just wanted him to stop hurting me for a minute. He said he would stop, he said he would be nice, he kissed me for the first time this week, but two minutes later, he fell asleep. So, yes, he was nice to me, but what that really means is that he was asleep. Does that count? He says it counts and even asking that question means I do not appreciate the respite from all the things he could be doing to me while he is asleep.

"Now don't make me rape you first thing in the morning," he said, choking me, "Bend over and take your fucking."

I did.

I moved too slowly at first and he pulled me from my end of the bed to his. He got on his feet and I bent over in front of him. The cane was still lying on his side of the bed, he picked it up and rapped against the pillow closest to my face. I pulled it to myself and buried my face in it. I wonder if there are people in the world who don't get through sex with silent screams delivered into memory foam that will develop PTSD by the time I am done with it. I clutched my palms with my fingers. Digging my nails into the expanse. His cock rubbed against my hole.

"You're finally not wet, anymore," he said, I don't know if it was approval.

"The lube is.." I started to respond, perhaps leading up to an apology.

"There is no need for that," he said, pushing into me with a violent burst of discomfort, "I can hurt myself a little to hurt you a lot."

He did.

He hurt me a lot.

I don't know when the Punjabi music stopped playing in the background of my life, but wherever I am now, it is a triumph that girl from the bar would understand. I made space for myself in the world, and in that space, I will be haunted as I fucking please. Tell me to hide my madness now, the glint in my eye is still fearless.

...

Tiny little droplets of blood splashed from my arms onto my face and shoulders. Every time he brought the cane down on my bleeding arms, more rivulets of scarlet decussated one another on my skin and poured onto the bed. I was chained in place, exactly where I go to bed each night, and I couldn't stop thinking about the very particular, eldritch romance of falling asleep on your own blood. Being lulled to slumber atop the plundered fields of your own massacre. I wondered if he was thinking about it too. He seemed so ensorcelled by the reactions of my skin, it felt like I had disappeared completely.

It's so strange, this condition where you are reduced to your flesh, not to be a sexual object, but one that bears endless pain. It's not even a reduction to the body, really, he reduces me to my suffering. I exist in all the ways in which I can hurt for him, do I even exist outside of my pain? Does he see anything else in me at all? Does he see that I am yearning for a moment of warmth? Could he tell, as he hit me, that I wished he could kiss my blood and then my mouth? Maybe he would have been able to tell if he wasn't so entrenched in the sanguineous seduction of my body.

He laughed, again and again, as he struck me and saw the blood pour out of me, he laughed. On any other day, in any other sequence of events, I could have really enjoyed this. I could have really enjoyed the handcuffs and chains around my wrists even though they were cutting into my skin. I could have enjoyed the cuts on my skin, burning from the exposure to the air. I could have enjoyed the impact of the cane on my arms as it came down, making my skin come alive with sensation. I could have enjoyed it. It seems like exactly the type of thing that would keep me warm on a lonely night, when memories and fantasy are all I have to wrap myself in. It seems like the sort of thing I would have tried to write into existence decades ago, when I was too afraid to believe in a fairy tale where *happily ever after* was forged in a dungeon.

But I suspect that something is broken.

This is the nature of unrelentingly persecution. It is not on the first day that you can take a person to the depths of their own horror, nor have them realise how pallid their resolve will become with prolonged exposure to despair, but on the tenth day, there is nowhere left to go. I'm at the bottom of the pit. Everywhere I reach, there is dirt and rubble. I avoid looking at it too closely because I worry that I will realise all of it broke off me.

I tried to turn my neck enough to look at the blood instead. I could see some of it, but not enough to placate the visual urge to see myself suffer. Then, almost out of nowhere, I started to beg him to stop. As far as I can remember it wasn't the pain, I wonder if I can really still even feel it. I felt a helplessness overcome me, a portentous helplessness, I needed him to show me he would care for me when I really needed it. I needed something, a single moment of compassion. I don't need him to bring me flowers, but if he could hold a dandelion out to me long enough for me to watch it fall to pieces, I will know that my powerlessness is not so abject I cannot escape. I will take a message sent to me in covert taraxacology, if he would just be willing to send me one. I begged and begged.

"You can beg all you fucking want, you cannot get me to stop," he said, swatting my wounds, "I don't know why you do this to yourself, why do you insist on holding onto hope?"

Why do I, though?

I suspect it is because it thrills me to see my naïve, little dreams crushed by his iron-clad resolve to destroy me. I suspect I give myself dreams I don't even want, just so he can shatter them.

It's the least I can do.

It's my dandelion for him.

...

Day 11

It feels like this began a very long time ago. My memory of the last week is nebulous, I cannot recall incidents, but I can recall sentiments. It is a maudlin memory. Yet it also, isn't. I feel detached from my worries of the previous week. They seem, quaint. You know how people who live in big cities visit little towns and think the difference in architecture and socio-cultural habits must mean that bucolic life possesses simplicity? My worries from last week feel *simple* in quite that way. I am projecting an aspirational simplicity on them that makes the present feel like it makes more sense. I find those worries so strange now. I was worried the world would come to an end because I allowed myself intense, decedent indulgence. I was so stressed because I overslept. I was so concerned that relaxation would teach me the lesson that it's okay to waste away and do nothing. Now I am worried about something else.

I'm not sure if I can get through this, but that problem is easily circumvented by him, I could only bring us this far, he has to take us the rest of the way, and I know he will, that's not my real worry. My real worry is that at the end of this road, I cannot go back to the place where we started or the person I was when we began. It's not all to do with these two weeks and the erotic structure of them. Far be it for me to pretend that two weeks of getting my ass kicked and my heart broken turned me into a different person. That's not how it works, but there is a reason why we do certain things in our lives at certain times. Sexuality, like everything else, is a construct that can help restructure your thoughts in a way that you can get more from them, like shuffling the letters of a word-finding game, but it is rarely the problem or the solution. It is not important what happened to me this week or the last, it's important why I chose to do this now. It was a declarative and performative act of transformation. I am not just ready to be a different person, I want to be as well.

The last eighteen-months of my life have been significant. I would say they were difficult but when I look back through them, I see less of a struggle and more of a process of comprehension. In all the time I have spent in all of these years worrying about being perfect, irrevocably productive, the most helpful, the most sorted, the least problematic, unwavering in my stability and tempered in all emotionality, I failed to see how much my systems of worry were a warning to start worrying about the right things. I didn't see it until a few things brought it to my attention. Well, two things. My natural response to professional success being a reason to hide and apologise was the first. My enthusiasm to make the lives of people who betrayed or hurt me easier by taking my emotions out of the picture and thinking only about their pain instead was the second. In response, I worried that I would stop doing things and working hard because having them be seen and appreciated felt so much like fraud. I also worried I would correct for being hurt by becoming a person who was incapable of trust or compassion. I was so worried about those two possibilities I doubled down on everything I was doing. I worked so much through the months of January and February, I started to lose my mind. I tried so hard to be a good, upright person, I started to undermine what I really am (which is not to say I am not "good," it is to say I was compelled to be inauthentic so I could still keep feeling like I was still a kind, compassionate person).

The truth is, and perhaps this is the truth for all of humanity, no matter how lofty and convoluted our thoughts, human pain and problems are pedestrian. I am just scared. That is all. I am scared of living in a world I cannot perfect — a world in which I will be hurt, I will win and lose, puppies will die and I will as well — and cannot control. I have been calling these weeks a penance, but that is the hook to get someone like me to do this kind of emotional work, it's really not about repentance as much as surrender. To him, but he is a symbol, we all are. This is my surrender to life. Life will happen. I will have to take it. Maybe I shouldn't worry I cannot go back to the world as it used to be, because when I really think about it, that's true every day. I cannot change that.

My heart is full of pain, but this curated, deliberate pain is a cushion I needed to put there, because I knew, I was about to fling myself, repeatedly, off the roof. Yet I don't feel anymore like I am falling, against all odds, I seem to have taken flight. The world is so hard, but everyday, it is laden with joy. With love. With sentimentality. With the endless opportunity to twist myself into knots to see what I become. There is no perfection to be had except for that. There is no perfection at all. There is no schedule but life and death. Everything in between could be freedom, if I let it be.

And I will.

...

He chained me naked to my desk while I worked. He chained me to the bed while I slept last night as well, but he does that a lot. We take intermittent breaks from chaining, but for the majority of the nights I have spent in his bed, I have been chained to it. This is different. He says I have to be chained and naked no matter where in the room I go from now onwards until the end of this period. If I am done with work, I have to tell him, and he will choose whether to untie and relocate me or not. If I need to leave the room or talk to someone who can see me, I have to ask, he will permit me to leave or dress, but I have to ask. I can dress if he permits me to leave the room, in which he says he will be locking me if he departs, I can dress, but as soon as I enter, I must get naked again. Usually, I am not comfortable with this kind of control over my life, the kind that spills over into spaces where I am completely autonomous — work, parenting, politics, society, other relationships — but I am not opposed to being subject to a temporary form of this control in the interest of supporting him to create a particular mindspace for me. I cannot do slavery with such regulation as the norm, not least importantly because this pedantic form of control is too time-consuming for its reward, but I am eager for it in intermittent bouts of intense adherence to an expanded code. With him, and really only him, I trust that it is not driven by actually wanting to turn me into a different person, teach me to be or live better, or usurp my agency. It's also because such detailed instruction and adherence only works if it is constantly witnessed, and without the complete presence of both people, in the way we are present right now, it turns into a list of tasks to undertake. I don't like task-based submission. I like ritual, but ritual happens, tasks are assigned. He is enabling my immersion and I appreciate it.

It makes my pussy throb.

I don't like to use that term, but I do use it sometimes. I call it cunt when it makes me feel powerful, I call it pussy when it makes me feel weak. When it is in pain or responding to pain, it doesn't make me feel weak, it makes me feel assaulted in strength, destroyed at my best and even when I succumb to the pain and accept it as a non-optional state of being, I still don't feel diminished. I still feel like I am in control of it. In arousal, though, it makes me feel weak. I cannot fight it and, slowly, like an insidious poison, it turns me into a creature of such basic need. It doesn't make me feel powerful, it robs of me whatever magnificence I see in myself that allows me to be confident, and replaces it with the most primitive of functions. It feels like it is no longer in my control, and then, the word *cunt* stops being the one that occurs to me naturally.

It feels like a pussy now.

My pussy is throbbing.

I realise I am no longer used to being naked all the time. Before the child came to live with us, and also back when I used to live alone, I was always naked at home. It had no meaning. My nudity was not a revelation but a constant condition. I'm still naked more often than the average person and I sleep naked as well, but it's different now. Now, I undress when he is going to beat or fuck me (or I am changing or showering). In the past ten days, especially, his instructions about my clothes have been very specific. Usually if I get rid of them at seven because he was touching me, I wouldn't put them on again until the next morning, even as our activities change. Now, he has been telling me, explicitly, not just when to take them off, but also when to put them on. I didn't realise that the instructions to dress and undress had become so intertwined in his intention for me that I was aroused by the instructions themselves until he told me I wasn't to wear clothes anymore inside our bedroom.

Now I feel so aware of my nakedness.

And my pussy is throbbing.

...

He chained me to the foot of the bed and locked me in the room, but first he fucked me. I finished working at my desk and told him so, he walked over to me and stood before me. He pushed me back into the wall as I sat at my bench and looked at my body. I lowered my gaze and let my hair fall around my face. He bent lower so his fingers could reach my pussy.

"Your cunt throbs for the wrong reason," he said, pushing his fingers inside me, one by one, bracing to fuck me with them like an unforgiving piston, "Put your arms up against the wall."

I raised my arms up over my head as he began to fuck me with his fingers, it felt uncomfortable to be in that position but not because of any strain it may have put on my shoulders, it felt uncomfortable to be positioned, in such specificity, for my punishment. It feels like more bodily exposure than just being naked. As he fucked me I got a cramp so severe in my abdomen that I fell off the bench and doubled over on the floor. After confirming that I wasn't injured, he let me writhe until the cramp had passed, and then he untied me from the desk and dragged me to the foot of the bed. He chained me back up and put his cock in my mouth. I thanked him before I began my usual devolution into the drug of its scent. I am expressing more gratitude than regret and amends today, I am expressing gratitude for everything, and it feels good. I know he likes it, he keeps trying to teach me gratitude, and then he keeps punishing me for not learning it, but this seems efficient, teaching me to be grateful for the punishment itself.

He fucked my cunt for way too long. My knee was resting against the chain once he bent me over the bed and by the time he was done, the impression of the chain had sunk in so deep, it looked like a permanent indentation. I had no determination not to scream or cry, but I had no impetus to scream or cry either. Despite being so loud on the inside, I felt so quiet as he fucked me. After he was done he made me clean myself off his cock and lick up all the cum that had dripped onto the bed. He smacked my face for getting his bed dirty, I apologised and thanked him for allowing me on the bed to be fucked. He asked if I had to pee and when I nodded he unchained me and made me crawl to the bathroom behind him. He held onto the chain as I urinated. It felt wrong, embarrassing, then he brought me back to the room and chained me up again.

Now he's gone.

And I am locked in here.

I wonder how long it will be.

...

There is very little noise left in my life. My concern that I would be unable to be productive or work hard if I engaged in indulgence seems to have been unfounded, I am more productive than ever, and it's taking me less than half the effort. I've suspended routines, bed-times, wake up times and fixation, but instead of leading to nothingness, it has led to cutting out all of the unnecessary noise that cluttered my life. I feel no need for the visual stimulation of Netflix, I feel no desire to scroll through marginally funny internet nonsense in order to fall asleep, I feel no need to participate in social theatre, I feel no active worries and I am literally filled to the brim with ideas and creativity. I do what I feel like doing and maybe it is the years of training myself, or the fact that despite my lapses in judgement every now and then, the general design of my life has never strayed too far from being who I really am and doing what I really want, but my world has not fallen apart by loosening my grip around my throat. On the contrary, I feel like I am doing better than ever.

I went for a run this evening instead of going to the gym, just because I feel I cannot be surrounded by people who might talk to me for the next few days, but also because the pool is going to open in fifteen days and I have to get my stamina back up to where I left it at the end of last summer. I made it to three kilometres last summer, I am determined to make it to five this summer. My swim partner from last year turned out to be a bit of a creep. It's not really like we were friends or that we even coordinated our schedules very much, but we generally swam at the same time, and we both did long distances, so we just started reporting to one another. He's about fifteen or twenty years older than I am, married and Bengali. His name rhymes with Sparta so I've been calling him Sparta for a year now. I think he misunderstood my friendliness to mean I want to fuck him, you know, as men do, and now it's uncomfortable each time I see him. He leers.

It is so disappointing when men cannot have a platonic or friendly relationship with you just because they see you as having crossed the social boundary of gender-compliant camaraderie as a sign that you must be a loose woman who wants to fuck them. It's enough to make you want to never befriend a man again, really.

Maybe I shouldn't.

Maybe I should fuck Sparta.

I fuck men to teach them a lesson sometimes. The lesson that they should be careful what they wish for, because they might get it, and they may realise, they cannot handle it. They should have befriended the monster when they had a chance. I can be scary if you cross me.

Boo.

...

I fell asleep chained to the foot of the bed on the floor while I waited for him. I keep thinking I shouldn't be this exhausted, but something about this is fatiguing. I kept reminding myself not to fall asleep, but I did. I curled my knees up to my abdomen for warmth and drifted off so easily. It's hard to believe it takes me hours of concerted effort to fall asleep in a bed each night. I woke up with a start because I felt something tapping against my shoulder.

"Who the fuck told you that you could sleep?" He asked, as my vision came back to me, "I left you here to wait, not rest."

I was on the precipice of offering an apology for my display of tiredness but he pushed me onto my stomach and swatted my back with the three-foot long bamboo stick he was brandishing. I kept thinking about that song, Chloroform Girl, and the sanguine expression and hymnal tone of the singer as he recited verses on verses about keeping a woman chained up in his basement. *Don't let me catch you sleeping again.* That song has haunted me before and at that moment, I couldn't precedent that it would haunt me again. It got stuck in my head, like an earworm and every single time he brought the stick down on my back, I started singing the chorus in my head, from the beginning, even if I hadn't gotten to the end. It started to drive me a little crazy, like the floor was spinning and I was walking in the opposite direction to keep the balance, as if I were on an acrobatic set designed by Yoann Bourgeois.

But I couldn't feel the pain.

I could hear the stick slamming against my back but I couldn't tell how much it was really hurting me, I may have asked him whether it was hurting very little or very much. He may have responded. Despite the absence of noticeable pain, I was terrified. I was more afraid than I have been on any other day, but I couldn't put my finger on the fear. I felt like I was chasing it around inside my head but each time I got close and leapt at it, it sprang like a mouse to the other end of the room, leaving me to crash face-first into the floor.

"If I asked you to stop, would you stop?" I asked him, all of a sudden.

"Are you asking me to stop?" He responded.

"I am not," I told him, "I just wanted to know..if I asked you to stop right now, would you?"

He was quiet for a moment. I am not entirely sure why I asked him that question. He has both told and shown me a hundred times over the past ten days that he won't stop.

"Yes," he answered at last, "If you asked, I would stop. Now you tell me, would you ask?"

"No, I couldn't ask," I replied as the fear started to make more sense, "I am not asking."

He continued to beat me and I started to cry. It felt like I had spent the entire day moments away from realising that if my captor left the door of the basement unlocked, I still wouldn't try to run and the moment of realisation dawned on me like an avalanche of tears. This entire day, all the hours spent locked inside the bedroom, naked and chained and assaulted, descended upon me in one fell swoop.

"Good," he said, "I would stop if you asked, but then I'd have to punish you for the guilt you would feel for asking, isn't it? It's best I keep beating you."

I straightened my back, got on my hands and knees and offered more of myself to him. Tears fell from my eyes straight to the floor. I cried until my eyes hurt even though I felt none of the pain in my body. How many tears are inside one person? I'm worried I'm about to run out of mine.

...

Day 12

I keep finding cuts and bruises on my body, ones I forgot and ones I never took note of, I can't tell if they are healing or forming. I don't care though. When I decided that I would capture a part of this journey visually, as well as in words, I was concerned about my ability to actually do it. It's not really that I am a bad photographer, I'm strongly okay, especially since I've had the benefit of some professional instruction (which didn't actually take, it was a struggle for me to pass that class and apparently you don't get extra points for essays as captions). I have a very poor visual imagination, I actually think I may have aphantasia, because when I do think, it's never imagery that passes through my mind, it's descriptions. When I think about people in my life, I don't see their faces, I remember their scents, the things they said to me, how they made me feel and what we did together. My dreams are rarely vivid or visual, they're mostly conversational and emotional, I don't remember seeing much at all, but I remember information being fed to me as descriptions and how it made me feel. When I watch things, I mostly listen or read the subtitles.

I remember the first time I had the — Do you think in words or images? — conversation with someone. It was my roommate Suzanne. We were sitting on the roof of our house, legs dangling over the side of the ledge, she was holding her blue guitar and talking, as always, about aliens. Somehow the conversation meandered to the point where she discovered that I wasn't seeing images in my head and I discovered that she was, we were both so surprised by one another's brains, I could not believe she had a picture book in her head and she could not believe I had a notebook.

"Our experience of the world will always be so different," she said to me, "You will never be able to think as me and I couldn't think as you, do you ever worry that you cannot feel what it's like to be other people?"

She gave me chills because I did worry about that. Well, maybe not worry, but I have thought about it with varying degrees of concern my entire life. I must have been around six or seven when I first started to panic about the fact that I couldn't embody the life experience of other people, when I attempted to ask my mother how it could be done, I realised the sentiment that was bothering me was very difficult to convey. She told me about empathy and maybe empathy was part of the answer, but my question and its origin was deeper than that, I didn't want to be able to understand other people, I wanted to be them. I wanted to access their consciousness. I didn't want to experience what happened to them, I wanted to *feel as them*. As a child, I really thought this was going to be one of the primary emotional and mental conflicts of my adulthood. As an adult, I realised this is why I write. Writing allows me to live a thousand lives, it comes naturally because the desire to *occupy* the life of another person preceded the expert instruction on the use of language, so the curiosity to discover was already in place. The obsession with self-awareness and the dissection of my own experience is to enable the granular comprehension of being human, so I may know what to look for, when I attempt to plagiarize the mind, pain and life experience of another.

It's not the same with pictures.

I take them because other people take them. I don't even take them actually, I have told my partners they can, so long as I cannot see the camera in action and I am not distracted from what I am doing and the space I am in. The camera is a disruptive medium to me. I understand that there are people who thrive in that environment, it is not an inherently disruptive medium, but when I see a camera, not just in a sexual scenario but even in a social one, I no longer want to do what I am doing. I no longer want to be there. I feel like I need to perform the moment. Any picture I do take myself, I take them after the fact when there is nothing left to ruin (not even me), but even then I do not enjoy it. I've said this openly before and I will happily say it again, I take pictures for the attention and the traffic so that people will see them and then go read more of my writing and subscribe. I barely did pictures before I decided to monetize my erotic content. I don't mind doing them for this reason, as a reason this makes sense to me, even though I don't like it but since it doesn't impact, change or hamper my writing in any way, I don't mind doing a slightly tedious task. I could just leave it be but I'd like to make more money because I'd like to make more money. If it hampered my writing or shifted my focus, I would stop.

As I set out to perform this two week journey into my own madness, I decided I would do a picture a day. I don't know why, it wasn't about the business aspect of this decision, I wanted to know what kind of picture I would take, if I didn't use the formula. In general, I use the formula: If you go to a mountain, take a picture of a sunrise, if you get a beating, take a picture of a bruise, if you stick a needle in your face, take a picture of the needle. That seems easy enough and even I can do it. It brings me no joy or thrill to share these pictures. However, in the past few months I have taken a few pictures that weren't formulaic, they were conceptual but most importantly, they were attempting to capture and convey an emotion. It was thrilling to share those pictures. I realised what I was seeking from making pornographic videos (in which porn is defined as sadomasochistic play) and I expected to hate it, but I didn't. I loved it. The thing I loved about it, aside from the fact that you can set up the camera and forget about it therefore taking away its disruptive power, was that it conveyed something I want to convey — Emotion, spontaneous interaction, vulnerability and humanity. There are no perfect angles in video, you kinda have to get them all. You can edit and direct, for sure, but let's say we are choosing not to. In video, I didn't have to curate or choose which parts of me I want to show and which ones I want to hide, in many ways it was very similar to how I feel about exposing myself through writing.

I write for a lot, lot more than exhibitionism, but there is an element of exhibitionism to my writing that I find sexually thrilling. It's the exposition of my dissected, vulnerable and emotional self. I don't actually want anyone to see me as a sexual goddess, I don't care to be found attractive, I enjoy the appreciation of a well-crafted sentence but that's a thrill for the trade, not my cunt. My cunt is thrilled to be exposed in pain and suffering. To my mind, the exposure of strength and beauty is recreational vanity (which is a perfectly fine hobby for anyone who enjoys it) and the exposure of weakness and ugliness is emotional pornography (which is my main hobby). When I am read, the parts of the exposure that entice me aren't the bits about my body, nor what is happening to me, but what I feel. Not my cunt, but my shame. Not my blood, but my terror. Not my tits, but my tears. Not my bruises, but my suffering. Not my screams, but my failure. Writing is the perfect medium for this form of exhibitionism, you can do so much with it and its primary component, words, are made entirely of history and sentiment. This may be a table but in my description of it, I can make you feel seven generations of my familial pain. In a picture of a table, that's much harder for me to do.

I suppose it is much easier for genuinely talented photographers and people who are adept at the visual medium, but for me, I couldn't relate to the expressionism of pictures for two reasons. The first is that the medium is too judicious, you give me to little to work with, when I have so much to convey and the symbols and metaphors that would be laden with meaning if I wrote them, are mere objects in photos. The second reason is that I never realised why I hated photography as a means of exhibitionism, it's clear to me now, it's because I didn't know what it is that really seek to exhibit. The very simple answer is my pain, but pictures of bruises and cuts aren't appealing to me and as I set out to find the exact nature of the kind of photo exhibition I would create, I found I wasn't interested in that at all. Not in costume, not in purple skin, not in staging. Not in any of the things I took pictures of earlier.

I found that I was looking to capture, as always, emotion.

I am not sure how successful I have been or will be at this, but if success is measured by whether I felt the erotic thrill of exhibitionism, I have succeeded a few times in the past eleven days. There were some pictures, not of sticks and blood, but tears and grimaces, that made me feel the same vulnerability and exposure I experience when I write or share videos. They made me want to hide my face and hold out my shame. They made me stare even though I wanted to look away. They made me feel like I had put my pain and suffering on the exact type of display that makes me yearn. Exhibitionism is so vast and so easily discounted as a sexual thrill. Exhibitionism may be half my sexuality, yet I prattle on about pain and suffering and nauseum, while form a corner, it watches, waiting its turn.

It's your turn.

I'm sorry to have kept you waiting, but you were harder to understand than you let on.

...

He held my mouth closed. He never does that. It is for the same reason as why he rarely ties me up, he doesn't want to force my silence or my stillness, he wants to compel it. He wants to demand it from my will. Sometimes while he is beating me, he tells me to hold my breath, that's what gets him off, the fact that I will do it, it wouldn't be hard for him to choke me, but he would much rather see the display of my compliance. When he held my mouth closed, it felt like an affront. I hadn't screamed, I wasn't groaning, all I did was whimper in response to his teeth on my neck and he slapped his hand onto my mouth so hard, my tongue stud hit my teeth.

"Enough," be growled, as if all these days of having to hear my pain had broken something in him.

He bit my neck harder, it felt like being consumed. It's strange for him to put his mouth on me as well. He never does that. I've seen him go down on other women, I've seen him passionately kiss other women, I've seen his deliver sensual nibbles and suck on nipples, but he has almost never done that to me. All my life, I have hated all of those things, I couldn't stand a single one of them, but his fervent denial of them to me has exalted the acts in my head. They went from being things I didn't enjoy to things I feel I am too broken to enjoy; they used to be undesirable acts, but his belligerent refusal to be willing to do them *to me and me alone* has made me long for them at times. He distorts my desire, like a catalogue that places a yellow couch so expertly inside a space, you think it would look just as good in your home even though you cannot stand the colour yellow.

A few months ago, in a moment of confusion and weakness, I asked if he would nibble on my nipples. He laughed at my audacity and then beat me for it.

"There is only one scenario in which I would put my mouth on your filthy body," he said to me as he whacked my face.

"Wh..at?" I asked, still harbouring vain hope, I suppose.

"To hurt you, obviously," he said.

It rarely comes to that. He has so many ways of hurting me, he rarely has to sully his mouth to do it. However this morning, maybe because he has already beaten me so much and so pervasively, there's room for other kinds of torture, so he bit my neck. He bit it over and over again until all of the skin started to burn, wear and rip. He held my mouth shut throughout the process, I beat my legs against the bed. My protest had more to do with the forcing of my quietude than anything else, it was like he was telling me I couldn't be trusted to adhere to his conditions anymore so he had no choice but to take action that circumvented my inevitable disobedience. When he stopped, he slid halway down the bed while I rubbed my neck to relieve some of the ache.

"I'm not about to find a wet cunt, right?" He asked, as he pulled my pants off me.

Even before his fingers had put their way to the mouth of my tired and abused hole, I was rambling from petrification. I feel constantly cramped, terribly sore and completely raw on my insides. I cannot take it anymore. I know I seem to say that every day, but I mean it every day, it seems to fall on a deaf heart and a dead soul. As he started to fuck me with his fingers, I struggled and closed my legs. These reactions are no longer in my control, I cannot even feign them by talking myself into it anymore. I have to hold my abdomen, like hugging a dusty teddy-bear after a fire, just to get through every single genital assault. I kept screaming the word no and he kept forcing his fingers in deeper, he is so crass with it, he could make it so much easier on me, I know that, because I have felt his fingers bring me so much pleasure as well.

"What the fuck do you keep saying?" He asked, coming to to me and holding my throat in his fist, "Are you fucking saying no to me, you brave fucking cunt?"

"Please," I begged, panicked by the lapse of my tongue, "Please."

"That's a better word, isn't it?" He asked, slapping my face, "That's a better word for you."

He lies. He would have done the same thing if I had said please as well. He just enjoys changing the rules and confusing me. Some days it's okay to say no but not please. Some days it's okay to call for mercy but not to cry. Some days he wants me to cry but not say no. He doesn't tell me which day is which, I don't think he knows either. He does tell me I am an idiot because I seem unable to learn that it doesn't matter what I do or say, there is no right or wrong, only his whim. Every reason and none is good enough for him to hurt me.

How will I ever be good then? I cannot. I suspect he doesn't want me to be either. He needs a bad slave because repentance makes him harder than reward. He wouldn't know what to do with me, if I stopped being sorry.

...

I found an old section of electrical wires in an old handbag, so he beat me with them. I told him a few days ago that I am worried it will be really strange to me when we go back to our regular schedules on Monday. When 11 AM rolls around will I crave my morning beating? How will I readjust to a reality where he isn't being horrible to me every minute of every day?

"You know what I love most about you?" He said in response, "Your Stockholm Syndrome is so, so easily activated."

It's not really Stockholm Syndrome, not really, because this relationship did not begin with a kidnapping or a confinement but there are elements of trauma bonding and the romance of hostility that make it seem like Stockholm Syndrome.

That doesn't make electric wires easier to bear on your legs. Nothing does.

...

By the time we got in bed, I was completely out of it. He lay beside me, on his side, and I lay on my back, holding my hands against my chest and fighting the stupor in my eyes. He was stroking my head and holding my hand, but every single time he moved even a little bit, I would shake and flinch as if he was about to beat me again. I cannot help it, the fear is bone-deep, I cannot stand it anymore. I've started to dread this bed and being in it with him. I've started to revile the night. I just want to sleep. For a few hours or days, I just want to sleep.

Before we got in bed he beat me like a savage. He slapped and punched my face until my lip busted open and started to spew blood all over the place. When he started it felt like a sexual interaction, like he was beating me, but it wasn't as destructive or cruel as the beatings that have come before this moment, but then he smacked me in the mouth with the back of his hand so hard, I lost comprehension of the world for a few minutes. I stared at him, eyes beseeching, begging for compassion, only to watch him come back to my face with his fists over and over again. The right side of my lip became so swollen that when he punched it, blood squirted into my mouth like a fruit gusher. His knuckles became drenched in my blood and in one moment, he pulled back and kissed it. He licked a drop off his knuckles and kissed it. It was the most romantic thing he has done in the last two weeks. For one split second, it felt like he still loved me.

I was telling him earlier that, sexually, he is the most disapproving man I have ever been with. I can do no right with him at all. He absolutely never calls me a good slave, a good girl, a good anything and I mostly appreciate it, but sometimes, when I realise that despite every effort I make to please him, he still tells me I am useless, it hurts so much. All these days I have suffered for him so dutifully and every day he tells me that I am useless and disappointing. I could sculpt my body with a knife and he would still punish me for the single hair out of place. It's who he is. It's who we are. But sometimes, a moment of reassurance, like kissing my blood, goes a long way. Three seconds after he stopped beating me I started to thank him when he started slapping me again for not thanking him.

"You don't even wait a second," I said, starting to cry at the unrelenting criticism, "I was about to say it."

"I shouldn't have to wait a fucking second," he said, pulling me by the collar, "You will fucking thank me before you start to breathe again, you will fucking thank me before you pass out, I don't care what state you are in, you'll thank me first before you die."

Damn it.

When we lay in bed later, my face still swollen and my lip still busted, I yearned for him. He was being tender and gentle, but quiet.

"Are you being nice to me deliberately?" I asked him.

"What is deliberately?" He asked, running his fingers over my mouth.

"When you..recognise that is what I need and you give it to me because I need it," I explained.

"Oh," he said, "Then, no. I'm being nice to you because I feel like it..right now."

I don't know why I asked questions that are bound to hurt, I could just accept the delusion and the momentary respite but I go looking for his cruelty instead. I wanted, so desperately for him to make love to me but I couldn't bear to be fucked the way he has been doing it. Maybe even for years. I just wanted to feel his warm body on top of mine, I wanted to feel his cock inside me, not ripping me apart and punching my cunt, but reaching for my insides in intimate passion.

"I want to feel you inside me," I started to tell him, but as he tried to pull off the covers I panicked and cried, "But please, no, please, don't fuck me I cannot take it."

He put my hand on his cock and I began to shake and cry. I begged and begged for him to not make me prepare the weapons for my murder, and he relented. That time I didn't ask whether the kindness was deliberate or not, I'll take the charity, if it means a few hours of safety. I'll take the alms of his pity. It's all I deserve.

...

Day 13

"It sounded like you were having nightmares all night," he said to me, a few minutes after we woke up.

"I don't really remember," I said, stretching in the bed as the chain rattled against the headboard, "I don't recall having any dreams. Really, I don't even remember when I fell asleep."

"Yeah you were out like a light," he responded, "I don't think you've ever fallen asleep hours before I did, but it has already happened twice this week."

It has happened twice this week, because I have been exhausted, but also, for the past two nights, I've tried to fall asleep the second my head hits the pillow because I'm afraid of being in bed with him. I am as afraid of his intentions as I am of how easy it is for him to inveigle me into championing my own destruction. In that regard, I am the perfidious one, he is always very honest about his intention to violate me. It is I who pretends that I am looking out for myself.

"I was really tired, master," I told him, "And I suppose, when I am asleep and you are, I feel safest."

"You think I won't wake you up to beat you?" He asked, "You think I won't wake you up to fuck you?"

I was concerned that saying yes or no would make him do it so I chose not to respond at all. He is not easily goaded but I worry nonetheless. Most days he wouldn't care if I believe he would do something or not, he knows it doesn't matter because I will likely not make the correct assessment anyway. That is true. When it comes to him, my judgement is genuinely unsound and often inaccurate. He is the person who knows me best, but there are alarming moments in which I realise that I don't know him nearly as well. I know who he is, I know about his life, I know his ATM pin, but there is another thing that is important to know about a person with whom you share an entire life. It's important to know what they are capable of, and with him, I don't.

Years ago he told me that before he first met me he thought I was a lot of bullshit and bravado. He's not the first person to think that about me and he won't be the last. My persona seems designed and curated to titivate, it is over-the-top in its intensity and people often assume or suspect there is something else, something less confronting and more human, underneath. As much as I would love to deny my humanness, it does exist, it's just on the surface alongside everything else. In many ways, I am not a deep person, because there is nothing on the inside that I don't wear on my skin. You don't have to dig deep to find me, that is not the challenge of me; I am not a hidden treasure nor an acquired taste, just a specific taste, that appeals to people who as kids used to eat chalk, pick their scabs and deliberately bruise their knees on asphalt. My outsides just seem hard to believe because most people keep most of themselves on the inside, but I keep everything of value to me in the garden and there is no gate. It's how I am with everything.

I reveal my own secrets out loud and not the salacious secrets of a sordid sexuality, those don't even feel like secrets to me, I reveal my struggles and fears. I reveal my ugliness. I reveal my intention. I don't make a display of revelation though, I just adorn myself in it. I reveal everything. I can see how it feels like too much. I can see why he thought it was a farce. I am used to being underestimated, or at least, suspect of performing an elaborate act of sophistry to finagle the world. I told him, back then, that it delights me to be underestimated.

But I was the one who underestimated him.

At least, there was on my part, a miscalculation in terms of his capability. It's been almost eight years since we have been together and even today I cannot tell what he is capable of. I cannot tell if he will actually do what he is threatening to do. In my head, he wasn't capable of the cruelty of the last two weeks, not to the extent that it has gone. Last evening, we were sitting at my desk and I was telling him exactly how much fear I have been carrying around, in talking about it I choked up with so much emotion, I cried.

"Don't you feel sorry for me?" I asked him, "Has nothing stirred your compassion?"

"I don't feel sorry for you," he said, his tone was acerbic but not unkind, "I love you, but my love doesn't guarantee compassion."

"Even now?" I asked, still crying as I blew smoke out of my mouth.

"Even now," he said.

I didn't know he was capable of that. In actuality, he doesn't need to pick up a whip or a belt anymore, he is hurting me, merely by existing, just by keeping me in this state of capture and reinforcing it with intermittent bouts of pain and emotional disregard. I am a minefield and he keeps throwing my own belongings onto me to test it. Sleep is the only respite.

"I'm sorry if I kept you up with my noises," I told him, preparing to get out of bed.

"No, I liked you having nightmares beside me," he said, unleashing me from his chains, "I'm pretty sure I gave them to you."

"Oh," I responded because there isn't much one can say to that.

"But I think I'll have to work harder, since you don't even remember them," he said.

The man I love is a stranger.

How is he capable of this?

I went to this church for absolution, I wandered around in the grounds and followed the sound of the bells, instead of a priest I made my confession to the sexton and now I'm buried alive in my own grave.

...

"Are you really that scared of me fucking you?" He asked me, moments after he had beaten and fucked me.

His question wasn't based on anything I did during the process, I am too broken to fight back, and the retinue of voices in my head that get me through life have all gone silent; so little of me has survived his expedition that I have gone quiet, which for my unrelenting garrulity is a departure from normalcy so severe, it's how you'd know I am not being myself.

His question is based on what happened last night.

Earlier, he was talking to me about how much he enjoyed my conflict from last night. I could sense it even then, as I stroked his cock and told him that I needed to feel him inside me, while simultaneously breaking into tears each time he made the slightest gesture that he may take me. I really did want him inside me, but I wouldn't have been able to bear it. My body would have survived, but my heart would not have returned from this journey. I told him that.

"You wouldn't have survived the lovemaking you think you want either," he had told me in response.

"You think you know what I want better than I do?" I asked, almost challenging to his authority.

"Yes," he told me, "My cruelty is harsh, you're struggling, but my tenderness would destroy you."

I hate it when he is right.

...

It's the thirteenth day and I am irked by the fact that it's not Friday. For a whimsical soul, I can seem quite like a pendant, but I swear, I'm not being pedantic, it's worse, I'm being superstitious. It's not the kind of superstition that is purported by any belief, it's the kind that I allow myself to foster because of sentimentality and a literary sensibility with which I decorate my life. It's the emotional equivalent of a beautiful sculpture of a naked woman in a yoga pose. It has some meaning, a little edge and no cosmic significance whatsoever.

I was born on Friday the Thirteenth and several of my most significant rapes also took place, not just on Friday the Thirteenth, but also my birthday. I am sorry to have put it like that, I know it's jarring to read someone who discusses their sexual trauma in a flippant, eroticised or ambivalent manner. It's easier to gawk in wonder of the coincidence that I lose my virginity to rape on thirteenth birthday, which was a Friday, and the thirteenth day of the month. The numbers are easier to deal with than everything else so I allow myself a little symbolism and wonder, a little macabre thrill. Many years later, when I finally dumped my former partner, on my birthday, which was also a Friday, he raped me as well. The next morning, after I had finished vomiting for an hour, I couldn't stop laughing about the way the dates had lined up. It was sad.

But somehow, after that, I began celebrating every Friday the Thirteenth that passed me by. I didn't really do anything in way of celebration except declaring that it was the birthday of my soul, but they began to excite me and each one that passed felt more special, like a rainstorm.

And now it's the thirteenth day.

But it's not Friday.

...

I asked him why.

When he asked me to spread my legs so he could fuck me with something, I asked him why. For a few hours now I've been wondering why I asked that question. It's not even about the audacity of questioning his lordship which I am sure was his problem with it, it's more the fact that the answer to my question was so obvious anyway. It was rather explicitly clear why he wanted to me to spread my legs.

And I asked, why?

I think I am losing my mind. He was indignant that I asked why, and expressed it in his classic manner of constantly looking like there's some garbage underneath his nose. How must it feel to be so disapproving all the time? I cannot relate, at all, to the thrill of controlling someone this way but I think I understand the exhilaration of being able to say certain kinds of things to another person. In polite society, you can't talk to people like he talks to me and for the sake of good, healthy relationships you have to communicate a certain way. You can't keep telling your wife she has a dirty pussy every time you touch her. You can't call her a disappointment ten times a day. You can't kick her to the floor and tell her she can't do anything right. You can't express these horrible, descriptive ditties of cruelty. Yet if you know you can create spaces where it's not only allowed, but relished, I can understand the allure of wielding that power.

I don't understand the motivation for the use of power in power exchange, but I understand the motivation of abuse of power. Everything he does to me is an abuse of power. I don't mean it is outside the realm of what both of us, in sound and analytical mind, agree to do with one another, I mean that in practice his exercise of power has no desire to do *good* at all. He doesn't want to teach, he wants to confuse. He doesn't want me to learn, he wants me to fail. And every once in a while if he does want to sculpt something out of me, he will never give me any approval for it, he doesn't care to offer any motivation to do things well. No matter what I do, he'll never let me be right or good.

I'm a bad slave.

Because he's a bad master.

But it's not a bad thing. What do we have to be good for? If fairness, kindness and compassion make one good, that's not what I'm looking for in my cunt nor my heart. I want a bad master, it's too late for me to be fixed with lessons, it's best just to punish me so I may atone for a fraction of my wretched soul.

...

I found out the origin of the term whipping boy recently. Evidently in certain monarchical kingdoms, it was not permitted to whip the royal children, so they were assigned a whipping boy instead, one who was raised alongside them so they could develop empathy and love for them. When the royal children misbehaved, their whipping boy was punished instead and the royal children were emotionally punished for causing such pain to their proxy-fraternal friends. That's gruesome. I wish I had never learnt that fact. Because it's the first thing that occurred to me when he brought the whip to the bed.

My favourite thing about whips is that every single time one strikes my skin, I want to stop immediately, but exactly ten seconds later I want just one more stripe and the cycle continues until I lose all track of self and time.

That's exactly what happened.

I didn't scream even once. I smiled several times. I didn't squeal or cry. I didn't clutch anyway. Really, I think it may be impossible to make me dislike whips. I realised while he was whipping me that I have never cried while being whipped. Maybe something about the whip makes me feel powerful. Maybe I just really like the sensation. It is the kind of pain that automatically suspends all the rest of my sexuality. I am no longer slave, submissive, horny or anything else, I am just masochist. That's why I cannot stop smiling. Each time the whip bites, I would close my eyes and a smile would just leak out onto my face.

He's been such a prominent part of everything I have been feeling, he has controlled everything I have felt every moment of every day for the past thirteen days but while he whipped me he disappeared for a while. Everything did, except me and the pain. It's like having sex with an old lover, not the kind who left pain or angst, but the kind who left the achingly soft familiarity of a well-used set of cotton sheets. Everything disappeared. He cannot punish me with this. Pain is on my side.

It's the thirteenth day.

I cannot lose on thirteen.

It's mine.

...

Day 14

Very little pain lingers in my body. You could cane me today and my thighs may appear swollen and purple, but it is unlikely that I will be able to feel it the next morning . You could punch my arms for hours, and I will cry as it happens, but two hours later, it will be as if it didn't. Of course, this will change somewhat as I get older, part of it is merely an accident of relative youth. I'm not *young* by any measure, but I can still get away with not washing the make-up off my face before I go to bed. I can still push a little harder than I should and trust there won't be any immediate consequences. Eventually, pain will linger in situations where it doesn't right now. The callousness with which I forget there are welts on my legs or a bruise on my cheek because I cannot feel them will be taken away from me. Right now, pain only lingers in specific situations.

I can access it if he makes direct contact with the area that is hurt, which is a fetish I contracted from him and it has become almost vital to my pleasure. The first beating just feels like the dress rehearsal and each subsequent interaction with the wounds feels like the real show. In that way, my pleasure can no longer be found in the moment, it is always in the future. The pain in my jaw tends to linger too, but I don't feel it at all for the first thirty-six hours after the beating, I don't understand why that is, but that appears to be my body's response time. The pain, always lingers in my cunt, and ever since I've been with him, it feels like it has only gotten more and more consistent and constant. I will never figure out his fixation on torturing cunts, it's not just me, he does it to everyone (with whom he is interacting sexually).

And pain lingers with whips.

My midriff still feels like it's on fucking fire. It burns to touch my skin, it still feels so warm, like it's preparing to bloom. I'm not particularly sentimental about cuts and bruises, my joy resides firmly in the experience when it comes to everything in the world, but there is something about the marks of a whip that makes me go back to the mirror, sporadically, lift my shirt up and admire.

Maybe it's because the pain lingers.

...

He keeps threatening me. There is no specificity to his threats, he just keeps telling me that I will wish for death this evening. He hasn't touched me all day. Well, aside from the fact that he fucked me in the morning, it's how he woke me up. I haven't been sleeping well. There were a few nights when I just crashed from exhaustion, but I was up by five most mornings. Alternately, I tossed and turned, unable to fall asleep most other nights, waking up to write and occasionally cry, at the oddest hours, only falling back asleep minutes before I was supposed to be up. Sleep has lost a lot of its allure even while retaining its role as the only space that feels safe from him.

And this morning, it felt like he was infiltrating that space.

The idea of being woken up with sex is such a popular fantasy, it seems like such a pleasurable way to start your day, but his cock pressing up against my ass this morning did not signal any pleasure at all. It was like being woken up with a death knell. His hand reached over my body and grabbed my sore abdomen, as he squeezed my swollen flesh, I pushed back against him in a trained response to please the cock. He leaned over to me and bit my earlobe.

"Good morning, slave," he whispered into my ear, "It's time to take your fucking."

I know what it means when he phrases it like that. It means that I should bend over immediately, put my hands behind my back and act like the receptacle he prefers his women to be during penetrative intercourse. The fear he has instilled in me for this act has grown exponentially and I am worried that it will never stop being as terrifying as it has become. My former partner instilled a similar fear of anal sex in me, I still cannot get through it without having a complete crisis of self and body. As he fucked me, I watched my hand, curled up on the side of my face, I watched it while he slapped my head and humiliated me for being a useless, disappointing cunt.

"Useless fucking whore," he growled as he shot his load into me.

It felt like a bullet right into my deepest wounds.

"I'm sorry master," I whispered into the sheets, it's all I know to say anymore, except the words he insists that he must hear and so I continued, "Thank you for punishing me."

...

He keeps asking me questions. The questions seem rhetorical, but in actuality, they aren't questions at all. They're statements structured into questions designed to offer information that is intended to terrify me.

If I sew your hands together in prayer, do you think you'll finally be able to earn your absolution?

I don't want absolution. That was never the point. The point was to titrate the effects of my own guilt-based neuroses so I could swim in the sentiment of repentance without being bogged down by the unnecessary shackles of self-loathing. The point was to allow myself to be sorry without the moral condemnation of needing to make amends. I don't care to be forgiven, he doesn't care to forgive me, really, neither one of us knows what it is I have done wrong. His question has nothing to do with absolution, he just wants me to know he has enough sutures to stitch my hands together in prayer. *I'll pray, my love, but there is still no God for me.* I'd be begging forgiveness from the void and I'd still have a better chance of being forgiven by the abyss than I have from him.

If the skin on your breasts is abraded, do you think you will be able to put on a bra for the gym?

He doesn't actually care if I am able to do so or not. The last time he took a stuff wire brush to my back, I texted him from the gym when I lay down on my back to do crunches to tell him that I was suppressing screams. He sent me a voice-note that contained nothing but the sounds of him laughing at me. These glib questions that roll off his tongue aren't designed to express any concern, he just wants me to know that he wants to peel the skin off my breasts and arrogate even more of my skin than he already has. *You can peel the skin off my breasts, my love, I'll still put on a shirt that hurts and sweat into the wounds without complaint.* If it hurts more to live my life because of him, then I'll take the pain, even in inconvenience. I'll call him and tell him when it hurts most, so he can laugh at me. It's the least I can do.

If I beat you with my belt over your whip marks, will that make new bruises or deepen the ones that already exist?

That question may seem like a scientific curiosity but it's one he has asked, answered and conducted several replication studies to confirm. He will always beat my bruises, in this realm his turpitude is nonpareil. When he sees me in tears, it will always spur him to more cruelty. If he sees me in pain, he will always desecrate that which is already broken. If he sees a massacre on my skin, he will pour kerosene on it and set me on fire. *You can hurt my pain, my love, that's why it exists.* I don't need him to bear witness to my suffering, I will build myself a soapbox to make an exhibition of my pain, I don't need him to pretend this state of brokenness compels him to care. With me, he can deracinate compassion from his soul, I will always take it. It doesn't matter if the bruises are new or just deeper, so long as he will always be there to make a bad situation worse.

If you start crying three hours before I am done with you, how much water would you need me to force you to drink to ensure you won't pass out from the dehydration?

I suspect he does care if I pass out. Despite his enthusiastic display of moral ambiguity, he does possess the capacity for sagacity. He just wants me to know he will make me cry a lot. I don't doubt that he will, it won't be because of the pain he causes my body, I know that too, it will be the heart-wrenching manner in which he stomps out any hope I dare display. I will display it too, if I have learnt anything it's that my resolve is mercurial, it is subject to the slightest changes in my emotional experience of him. I may decide to be perfect, but it doesn't matter what I decide, my illusion of will is ephemeral. *But you go right ahead and make me cry as much as I can bear, my love.* I need his facilitation of my tears like an addict needs their next fix. I will pour my life onto his floors, I will show myself in the weakest and most exposed state that I can embody. I want him to see me like that. There is a beautiful song in which the singer, addressing a former lover says: *'Bichadte waqt un aankon me thi humari ghazal, ghazal bhi aisi jo kisi aur ko sunayi na thi'*, a literary translation of which would be — *'In the moment of separation, the eyes of my lover read back my own poetry to me, and it was poetry I never revealed to anyone but him, poetry he inadvertently came to own.'* My tears are the poetry I never reveal to anyone else, they're his. I want him to have them until I run out and then I will make more just to satiate his hunger for my suffering.

I will build myself in structures of pain, my love, to give to you.

...

Why do you keep beating me?

He brought his belt down against my back and it felt worse than anything in the world. My barometer for the measure of pain is completely warped. Yesterday, as he whipped me with a bullwhip, I didn't make a sound, it didn't feel excruciating even though my skin was changing colours right before my eyes, it felt beautiful. In comparison with the whip, the belt should have felt like nothing, right?

But it's not that.

I hate the climax of everything. I hate grand finales. I hate the pressure of the end of storytelling. The reason why I dislike films and thrillers or mystery novels is that there is so much riding on the exposition that it's impossible to do right. You know that show — I May Destroy You — I liked part of the conceptual direction they took in the finale. They did three possible endings, and I would have loved it if they had left it at that, but so harsh is the expectation of a perfect ending, that they hedged and included the *real* ending as part of the finale as well. I wish they hadn't done that. Often, when I watch or read endings, I can see the hand of the writer being forced to create something explosive. To end with a big bang.

I don't like bangs.

As he beat me, having laid out a dozen things with which to hurt me, it felt like a bang. I could not bear it. I started to cry five minutes into his belt being administered onto my back. As I cried, I expected him to be more compassionate than he has the past two weeks, I realise that I refuse to learn, I refuse to abandon irrational and naïve hope, but that is who I am. Every day, I wake up and I try to fix things in the world, I know it's distasteful to say that about one's own self but I don't know how to describe my job without saying that, if I let myself abandon hope and optimism, I would never be able to do my job again. I have spent the past year being more perturbed and hopeless than ever before, you get knocked down and sometimes it compels you to stay down, and I figured it was time. It was my time to learn that you cannot trust anyone, the world is a horrible place, you will never get what you think you deserve and there is no joy but moments stolen from the unforgiving grips of life.

But I was wrong to think I could be that person.

The fact that I refuse to abandon hope for his tenderness is not a tragedy, it's a triumph. Hopelessness is not a lesson I want to learn again. In the past year, I have clutched to my routines and my schedules more than I ever have before, I explained to myself that it was because I had more work than ever and organisation always helps to manage time better. It's not entirely untrue, I am genuinely fond of efficiency to the point that nothing turns me on more than an efficiently-managed situation, but my growing obsession with it was not about my fondness. It was about the fact that I was disillusioned with everything I have been doing in life. All of it — the inability to feel accomplished, the reluctance to celebrate anything, the constant diminishing of everything I did — was stemming from the fact that I had started to lose hope. I had lost hope in the people in my life. I had lost hope in my ability to affect any real change. I had lost hope in the world. I was drowning in the noise and clutter of mindlessness that litters the world under the garb of décor. I had to clutch to routine because it created the illusion of belief.

I don't want to clutch anymore.

I want to believe in things, against all odds. I wanted to believe that he would stop hurting me. I didn't scream or should as he beat me, I didn't fight him or attempt to establish a circumstance where he didn't use every single one of those items he had placed on the bed. The belt, the knife, the needles, the scalpel, the oven brush. I had accepted the condition that he would use each one on my body until it was even more desecrated than before. I didn't want to stop it, I just wanted to cry because his relentless pursuit of me was weighing so heavily on my body, I had to release some of the pressure lest I collapsed under my own weight. I wanted to cry because despite all acceptance, you can still hope for a better tomorrow. Hope is free. Hope is cheap. Hope is abundant. Hope of a difficult choice.

I chose hope.

I cried as he stuck a needle in my back and howled even more when he wouldn't stop telling me that I was still being a useless, disappointment. I cried as he swung the belt against my back with vehement force to punish me for my tears. I cried until I wet the bed, until my nose was completely blocked, until all of the accumulated angst inside my soul was pouring out through my eyes.

"Why do you keep beating me?" I asked, intermittently, but it wasn't meant for his ears as much as it was for mine.

I didn't need to know why. He did not need to tell me, but the helplessness made me question the circumstances of my plight.

Why do you keep beating me?

"Do you want me to stop beating you?" He asked me, pulling me up by the hair and looking into my eyes.

I could not say anything. I could not say no because it wasn't the truth, I did want him to stop. I could not yes because it wasn't coming from an honest place, I wanted him to stop, but more than that, I wanted it to not matter what I want. I wanted to have hope, not choice.

"I don't want it to be my choice," I finally mustered through my sobs.

"Good," he said, patting my head roughly, "You don't choose, you don't ask, I told you, you just take what I give you."

"Thank you master," I told him, and for once, those words of gratitude may have been more a function of meaning than habit.

"Get on the floor, on your knees," he said, pulling me off the bed and onto the floor.

He sat on the edge of the bed and I kneeled between his legs. My hands folded themselves before him and he put down the belt and held both of them in one hand.

"I won't beat you anymore," he said, and I started to wonder if he had anticipated any of this.

"Thank you master," I said, before launching into a tirade of tears so strong, they could have uprooted our house.

He pulled my head to his knees and let me cry until my legs went numb. He didn't reassure me. He didn't tell me it was okay. He didn't express any approval nor disappointment in me. He just let me cry. It had none of the flavour of a finale, but in my head the perfect ending isn't a bang, it's silence.

In the end, there was silence.

...

Printed in Great Britain
by Amazon